The NEBADOR series:

Book One: The Test

Book Two: Journey

Book Three: Selection

Book Four: Flight Training

Book Five: Back to the Stars

Book Six: Star Station

Book Seven: The Local Universe

Book Eight: Witness

Book Nine: A Cry for Help
2015
Book Ten: Stories from Sonmatia
2016

Also by J. Z. Colby:

**Standing on Your Own Two Feet:
Young Adults Surviving 2012 and Beyond**

NEBADOR

Book Eight

WITNESS

an epic young-adult science fiction adventure

by

J. Z. Colby

and the short story

The Magic Needle
by Kathleen Tully

Nebador Archives

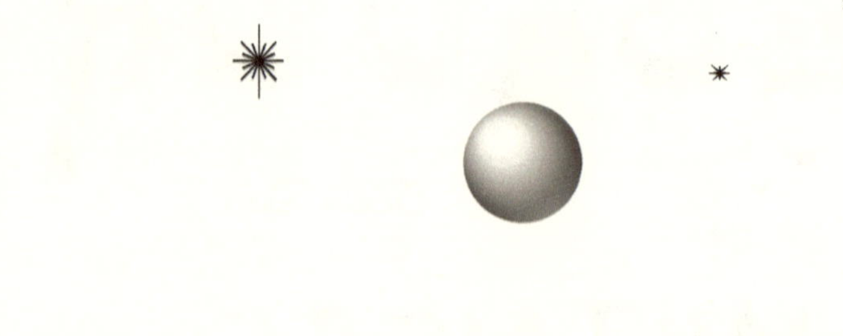

Copyright © 2014 by J. Z. Colby
All rights reserved

Cover art by Rachael Hedges

Illustration by Sidney Oster, and children's drawings by Meghan Paige Williams, Jessica Williams, Floyd Bourland, Jeff Bourland, Anne Marie Beltzer, Steven Beltzer, Trentina Porter, and Nathaniel Exum

For other print editions, ebooks, dramatic audiobooks, previews, samples, biographies, comments, questions, artwork, writing contests, Ask Kibi advice, deep learning notes, Nebador citizens, and more, please see:

www.nebador.com

Nebador Archives
Kelso, Washington, USA

Library of Congress Control Number: 2014910385
Manufactured in the USA

ISBN: 978-1-936253-76-0
NEBADOR8PBG: paperback, 6" x 9", 187 pages,
    global edition (10-point Georgia type)

**Dedicated to Peter James, the psychic investigator,
and a girl whose name may have been Jackie,
who may have died in the 2nd class swimming pool
on the R.M.S. Queen Mary.
Also dedicated to Gian and Sophia Temperilli,
and Erika Frost,
who carry on Peter's work,
each in their own way.**

Greetings, young people of planet Earth,

This story is special. I had all the usual help from the Muses, and also some specific nudges and whisperings from a certain little girl (see dedication above). Unfortunately, I cannot share royalties with her, because of her current immortal state, and even her name is not known for sure. She stuck something in my shoe last time I was visiting her "home," and it is now one of my most cherished possessions. I hope it will allow her to find me if she ever needs to, and I will visit her as often as I can.

That same little girl seems to have known where the NEBADOR series was going, for the "darkness" she injected into *Book Eight* was just right to prepare me, and hopefully my readers, for *Book Nine*. Some young people, of course, shy away from "dark" stories, and some parents try to protect their children from such stories. That's okay, as the "darkness" we are moving toward may only allow passage by a few.

J. Z. Colby
2014

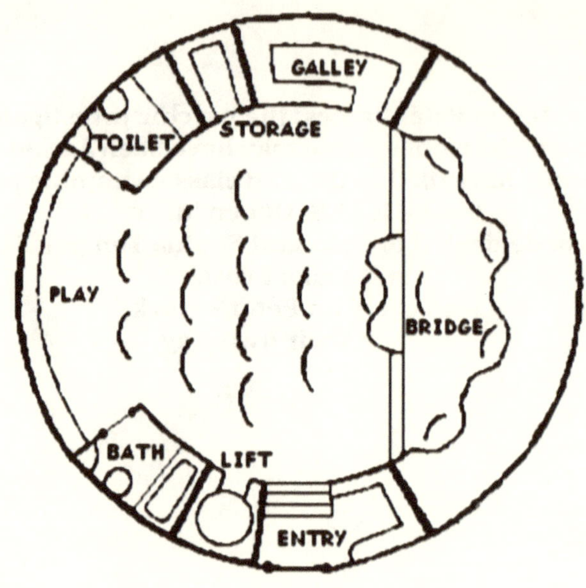

Acknowledgements

Wonderful people throughout the author's life provided unique and irreplaceable lessons and inspirations:

Juniper Russell
Vicky Ball
Linda Dezzutti
Jennifer Carolyn Gates
Rachael Bleich
Paula Wells
Sarah Satterthwaite
Ashley Riddle
Antonya Pickard

Esther Smith
Dottie Frisbie
Martha Higgins
Susanne Koller
Charleen Cox
Meredith Herzog
Patricia Sharp
Peter James

Valuable readers gave the author feedback after digging through early drafts of the book:

Karen Oster   Cecelia Harper

Excellent critiquers commented on thousands of passages, then provided reactions during in-depth interviews:

Sidney Oster, 13   Dylan Oster, 14
Catherine "Cat" Harper, 15   Joshua Utter, 18
Alex Chalcraft

Careful publishing assistants, proofreaders, and technical helpers brought the final manuscript as close to perfection as possible:

Cecelia Harper

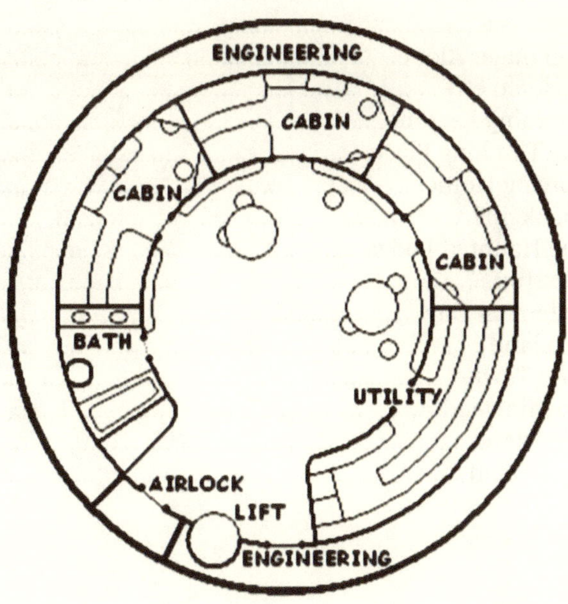

Contents

"What the caterpillar calls the end of the world, the master calls a butterfly."

— Richard Bach

Chapter 1: The Education Service

The monkey-mammal girl stood alone in the waiting room of response-ship dock D-Twelve on Satamia Star Station. She could see the spherical ship Manessa Kwi, through the clear walls, as it carefully entered the blue and purple docking fingers. A moment later, the boarding tunnel began moving toward the ship.

Ashley was excited about having lunch with her friends, and felt no need to hide her facial scars, as the crew of the Manessa Kwi knew all about the events, back at Lyceum on her home planet, that had caused those scars.

But she frowned when suddenly, just as the boarding tunnel made contact with the golden ship, several people from the medical center came striding into the waiting room, some with floating stretchers. She quickly stepped to the side, out of the way.

She was still having a little trouble thinking of birds and reptiles as "people," but it was getting easier, especially because most of them were smarter than her, and nearly all of them far more experienced. She loved her new home so much that she was determined to succeed. Anyway, she had always had a hunch that people — that is, human beings — weren't quite as important in the universe as they liked to think. Now that she was here, she knew her hunch had been quite correct.

The huge spider, last to enter the waiting room, caused Ashley to swallow, but she quickly noticed that it was in charge of the medical team, and even Dakalio, the only human healer on Satamia Star Station, was listening carefully to the spider's instructions.

As soon as the ship's hatch opened, stretchers floated in, and soon came out with bandaged ursines and avians. A reptile who walked upright came next, supported by Healer Dakalio, its arm in a sling and a bandage on its head.

The spider quickly examined each person with the help of a hand-held instrument, then waved them along.

Finally, when all the healers had departed with the wounded, the crew of the Manessa Kwi emerged. None were injured, but they looked like they hadn't slept, eaten, or washed in days. They hardly noticed Ashley and flopped onto couches or the soft floor itself, sighing or moaning with relief.

Ashley was suddenly very glad she had chosen the Education Service instead of the Transport Service.

*

A few minutes later, a large beetle arrived with a tray of nutrition drinks. "I've marked Manessa out-of-service for a day," he said.

"Thanks," Kibi said from the floor. "The ship needs *everything*."

"We do too," Sata said from a couch, reaching for a cup. "Hi, Ashley."

Seeing that the crew had no other immediate needs, the beetle departed.

Ashley noticed there were seven drinks, wondered how Nebador . . . um, people . . . always knew these things, and grabbed one. "Looks like you guys had a tough mission."

"It wasn't *supposed* to be," Ilika said from a couch, his head nestled in a pillow.

Boro, still on his back on the floor, sighed. "At least no one *died*."

Rini chuckled. "I think they came close a couple of times."

"Too close," Mati declared before taking a long pull from her drink. "You're pilot, next hard mission, Boro,"

He swallowed. "Um . . . that's fair, I guess."

Rini laughed again. "Yeah, next time we get another Education Service mission, we'll know to stock extra medical supplies!"

Ashley's eyes snapped open wide.

*

After a Satamia day of rest, the crew was busy cleaning and re-stocking their ship, chatting about tense moments during the last mission as they worked, when Arantiloria appeared and swirled into her purple-haired human form.

"In a few days, you have another Education Service mission . . ."

Boro moaned from the floor as he guided a hovering machine over the blood-stained carpet.

". . . but this one should be without any dangers or injuries."

"Whew!" Kibi breathed from where she sat on the galley counter, unloading boxes of food packets.

Ilika poked his head out of the toilet room, long-handled brush in hand. "That'll be a nice change."

"But there is some training I want you to complete," the spirit continued, "before you get that easy mission, training that will — what's that saying from Sonmatia Three? Oh, yes — curl your toes."

Sata slid out from under the navigator's console. "I *knew* it was too good to be true!"

* * *

Chapter 2: Advanced Training

Mati plopped down on the top step of the entryway, tears streaming down her face. A moment later, Rini appeared at her side and wrapped his arms around her.

At the engineering station, Boro sighed and shut down his engines. As soon as he rose from his chair, Sata stood near, eyes glistening, almost a pout on her face. They shared a tender embrace, then walked hand in hand to the large oval table in the passenger area.

Kibi, still in the command chair, kept her face hidden in her hands for another minute, then slowly collected herself and stood up, shoulders slumped, feet heavy as lead. Seeing that she was now alone on the bridge, she dragged herself up to the table.

Ilika silently set a plate of finger food and cartons of juice on the table, then calmly took a seat.

After a few more minutes of awkward silence, Mati and Rini joined the others at the table.

Kibi took a deep breath. "What'd we do wrong, Ilika?"

A half-smile crept onto the captain's face. "How do you know you did *anything* wrong?"

Several of the crew members looked at each other.

"Because ..." Boro began after swallowing the gotaka nuts he was chewing, "we *crushed* eight of the furry creatures we were *supposed* to rescue, *scared* the pee out of the rest, and managed to save exactly *five*, out of three or four *hundred!*"

"And those five were all *males*, so they'd go *extinct* in a few years!" Sata added, nearly gasping for breath.

As the pilot who had caused the death of several of the little creatures, Mati was about to open her mouth and express her frustration when she noticed the moisture in Ilika's eyes. She swallowed her thought and took several slow breaths before she spoke. "You've had to do this kind of simulation before, haven't you?"

Ilika nodded. "And even though we get better at it, it's never easy."

Rini squeezed Mati's hand. "So . . . please tell us how we can do better."

Kibi nodded. "Part of me wants to run to the nearest knowledge processor and ask to be a dishwasher or tree trimmer or something. But ..." She paused and took another slow breath. "But, I know it's just how I feel right now, and after you teach us some new things, we'll be able to do it."

"We've always wanted to rescue people and animals," Mati said. "Remember what we wanted to do back at Cattle Town?"

Ilika smiled at the memory of Buna asking to borrow his bracelet to put all the slave traders to sleep.

"We just never realized how *complicated* it could be," Mati concluded.

"I think we started to see that a little bit after taking Timod Gor home," Boro suggested, "but we obviously need to learn more."

Ilika let a few moments pass to see if anyone else wanted to speak. The silence lengthened, so he collected his thoughts. "The most important lesson you must learn is that there is NO perfect solution to any problem that involves a desperate situation, emotions running wild, and the free will of other creatures . . ."

"A sun exploding," Sata began, "with eight minutes to rescue an *entire* sapient race, is about as *desperate* as it comes!"

Ilika nodded.

*　*　*

Chapter 3: Another Try

"Seventeen," Ilika reported, fulfilling his duties as acting steward, but leaving Kibi in command. "About three-quarters male, half old, half middle-aged, except for that one infant."

As he spoke, the seventeen fluffy white mammals with long pink ears, sitting on the floor in the passenger area, all changed back into fuzzy blue balls of light, then disappeared.

Mati finished with her console and spun around. "That's a *little* better. At least they wouldn't go *completely* extinct. You were right, Rini. The minute of rescue time we lost, by moving away from their main plaza, was worth it. We only crushed one."

"I'm lowering the table," Ilika announced, then stepped into the galley. The others came up from the bridge.

Sata slid into a chair. "We really have to find ways to avoid hurting *any*. The moment one screams, most of them run away scared."

Ilika remained silent as he placed snacks on the table. Boro grabbed a chair beside Sata.

Kibi chuckled dryly. "It feels funny for *me* to be saying this, but the name of the game, to rescue these beautiful little creatures, is to avoid *any* emotional reactions."

Ilika flashed her a smile.

Rini's face suddenly twisted with thought. Everyone noticed and looked at him.

"Manessa," he began, looking at the ceiling, "can you stretch your hull in a couple of places to look like bunny ears?"

"Yes."

"Can you make the ears pink, and the rest of your hull white?"

"Yes."

Ilika raised his eyebrows. "I don't think *that's* been done before. It's worth a try!"

*

As Manessa knew she should, she waited for an awkward moment to begin the next simulation. Rini had three items on the stove in the galley, Kibi was taking a bath, and Boro and Sata were sharing a deep kiss in the engineering ring on the lower deck.

"Emergency mission, supernova detected, one sapient race vulnerable, transit time fourteen minutes, complete planetary incineration in twenty-four minutes. Prepare for star transit."

The crew had that much memorized. They all got comfortable where they were and cleared their minds. Rini had the biggest challenge, first touching the stove's shut-down symbol, next tossing his knife into the sink, and finally plopping onto the floor to enter the meditative state that would protect him from insanity during the timeless and spaceless experience of star transit.

What seemed like a second, but might have been a year later, they popped back into space and time as close to the doomed planet as possible. Mati was quickly at her station, yelling for engines with voice commands to the ship. Boro arrived a moment later and took over the process, adjusting power levels he knew his pilot would want, and preparing alternate fuels just in case.

The star had already exploded, the daytime side of the planet was nothing but molten rock, and the nighttime side was rapidly changing to ash and cinders as the planet continued to turn on its axis.

Even though she had already done the simulation twice before, Sata's entire body was covered with sweat as she focused her mind on finding the right planetary chart and marking their destination, a cave and tunnel system where about four hundred sapient mammals lived, the last such cave, out of thousands, that would rotate onto the daytime side of the planet and be instantly burned to a crisp.

The pilot breathed a little easier when the chart flashed onto her screen. "This time I'm gonna try to avoid crushing *anyone* by stopping eight meters above the plaza, *then* moving to the landing field."

"Good idea," Kibi said from the command chair, her hair still dripping wet. "You ready with that shape and color, Rini?"

"Manessa's gonna be the biggest bunny rabbit they've ever seen! It's all programmed and on Mati's console."

"I see it," Mati said. "Prepare for emergency de-orbit at ion three."

"Ion three, anti-mass seven, full inertia canceling, maneuvering thrusters," Boro confirmed, knowing exactly what his pilot needed, and what else she would call for soon enough.

"Next stop, one thousand meters above ground level," the pilot said as she glanced at her status screen and touched the ion drive symbol.

The planet, surrounded by the intense glare of a sun now half the size of the planet's orbit, swooped toward them. Kibi, looking straight ahead at the main bridge screen, had to close her eyes for a moment to avoid dizziness.

Most of the nighttime side of the planet was cinder-black and glowing red in places, especially near the left edge where the land had recently rotated around from the daytime side. But along the right edge, a crescent of land still showed hints of brown, green, and blue, lit up by the intense light streaming through space all around the planet. Even as they approached, the habitable crescent was shrinking.

Suddenly their display ceased rushing toward them, the dimly-lit land only a thousand meters below.

"Ion one to eight meters," the pilot announced.

"Freeze simulation," the captain said from the steward's station. "Sorry, that's only possible because you've verified the land elevations during a previous run. That wouldn't be the case in a real situation."

Mati snapped her fingers. "Ion one to one hundred meters ..." the pilot proposed, then turned to look at her captain.

He smiled. "Continue simulation."

"Ion one," the engineer verified.

The ground rushed toward them again, allowing the crew to clearly see the plaza and cave entrance in the eerie twilight. Mati quickly covered the remaining distance with maneuvering thrusters, and while doing so, touched the special shape and color symbol Rini had programmed.

White furry creatures, about a meter tall when they stood up, began pouring out of the cave, gazing at the strangely-glowing sky and the white and pink ship that just appeared above their plaza. Some eyes swirled with fear, but most were simply in awe. A few knelt down and raised their arms to the sky. More quickly joined in.

"I think ... they're worshipping us," Kibi said. "Is this what you had in mind, Rini?"

"No. But if it gets them into the ship ..."

"I'd crush a hundred if I landed here," Mati said as she moved her flight control. "Okay, little bunnies, follow the big bunny in the sky to the field."

Even though the little creatures were quick on their feet, the ship was quicker, and Mati had struts on the ground before the first furry mammal arrived.

"Sunrise, and the end of the world, is in seven minutes," Sata announced, "from right . . . NOW."

A count-down timer appeared on every display.

"Passenger area is ready," Ilika announced, "ramp out, hatch open."

Kibi jumped to her feet. "Manessa, close the hatch at eight seconds on the timer no matter who is in or out."

The deep-space response ship confirmed the order.

✳   ✳   ✳

Chapter 4: New Insights

Do you think it's going to work? Arantiloria, currently invisible to all mortal eyes, asked the deep-space response ship.

According to my memories of this and similar training simulations, and a couple of real rescue missions, the steps they have taken to reduce the fear of the local population should result in a moderate improvement in their success.

*

"Twenty-one," Ilika announced as everyone gathered at the table and grabbed juice cartons to quench dry throats. "Again, mostly male, and mostly old."

Boro growled with frustration. "We could squeeze *that* many into one of the toilet rooms!"

Sata laughed, imagining bunnies piled in a bath tub.

Rini smiled. "I noticed they were different ones from the last time. Before, I think we got mostly political leaders. This time, we got religious leaders. I declare my bunny-in-the-sky trick a complete failure."

Mati looked at him with sympathy. "It was a *slight* improvement. But leaders of barely-sapient creatures are usually gonna be old, and male, just like in our kingdom."

After a long silence, Kibi finished carefully chewing and swallowing a cracker. "We're doing something basically, fundamentally wrong, aren't we, Ilika? We should be able to get one or two *hundred* of those little creatures into this ship."

"This is one of those exercises that would be worthless if I gave you the slightest hint. Believe me, the pride and confidence you will feel, when you succeed, will be worth all the frustration."

"But what if it takes us an entire Satamia *day?*" Sata said, trying not to whine.

"I have a feathered friend whose crew wrestled with this simulation for *three* days! If anything, you guys are ahead of schedule."

Sata took a deep breath and almost smiled.

✳

Arantiloria silently observed the next two simulations.

I knew they were ready for something different, but I didn't think they'd try the social approach so soon.

Most mammalian and avian crews try it fairly early, the ship replied, *but the reptiles and insects usually wait longer.*

I didn't realize humans were a race who tended to over-estimate their charms so much, Arantiloria mused.

That is beyond my understanding.

What did you think of Sata tossing fresh vegetables onto the ramp?

It reminded me of an avian crew that put out seeds and nuts for the same purpose. The simulated victims, in that case, were other birds.

Arantiloria smiled to herself.

✳

Sata whimpered with frustration as she landed in a chair at the big table. "And I wasted all those good vegetables for nothing. We could have made a stew."

Boro sat down close beside her. "We have to try things, or we won't get anywhere."

Kibi sighed. "What was the count, Ilika?"

"Sixteen, but only about half were males."

Boro moaned again. "Rini's bunny ears worked better."

"Hey!" Kibi began, trying to cheer him up. "Remember what happened when I went out to talk to them?"

Sata pouted a moment longer, then smiled. "They . . . um . . . ran."

"All but two," Mati remembered. "Yeah, we're doing something very wrong, one of those things that's gonna be hard to think of because it won't . . . you know . . . feel right."

Rini noticed a slight smile appear on the captain's face. "I think you're on the right track, Mati."

When Mati remained silent, Sata took a deep breath. "So . . . how do we think of something that's . . . too weird to think of?"

✳

After Ilika tried to comfort them by announcing that only half a Satamia day had passed, and Kibi realized with alarm that they hadn't slept in more than two ship-days, everyone filtered away to get some rest.

Ilika had barely closed his eyes, it seemed, when he was awakened by Kibi dancing around the cabin, turning on lights and using the knowledge processor, seemingly all at once.

"Of course, of course, of course, it's so simple! Why didn't we think of it sooner? Actually, I know why. *We* hate not being in control of our lives, *we* think we can solve any problem that comes along, so we think *other* creatures should be able to, also, even when the situation is *completely* outside their experience!"

Ilika propped his head on one hand to listen.

"Of course, *we're* no better at it than the sapient bunnies, but we *think* we are, so we think *they* should be. I want to do another simulation," she asserted, reaching for the knowledge processor.

"No!" Ilika commanded. "Not until everyone's had a few hours of sleep."

Kibi pulled her hand back, but was still bouncing with excitement.

"Come here. You obviously aren't going to get any more sleep, so I'll keep you occupied."

Kibi looked at her lover and could see the passion in his eyes. She took a few more breaths to settle her nerves, then turned off the lights. When she felt his hands in the dark, she giggled and relaxed.

* * *

Chapter 5: The Imperfect Solution

Did you see Kibi's dream? Arantiloria asked Manessa.

No. I do not have that ability.

It was beautiful! She had all the pieces of the puzzle floating around in her mind, and as soon as she drifted into sleep, they came together. She doesn't remember the dream, but it was quite bizarre, and left her with a clear understanding of what they were doing wrong. No rational, logical thought process could have accomplished that.

The avians dream also, from what I've seen, the ship said.

That opens up some wonderful possibilities for passing bits of information and wisdom to them when they get stuck and need a nudge.

You can do that?

✳

Kibi was nearly bouncing with excitement, and had difficulty letting the others finish breakfast before standing up at the head of the table. They chewed their last few bites as they listened.

Kibi started with a slight cringe. "You're not gonna like what I realized last night."

"Don't worry about it!" Boro said firmly. "We don't like the numbers we've been getting, and we all feel like failures, so we'll try *anything* that might work."

Rini, Mati, and Sata all nodded.

Kibi cleared her throat. "We've been ... how do I say this ... treating them like *we'd* like to be treated, but the truth is, we wouldn't have the *slightest* idea what to do if our sun went supernova, and neither do they."

After a long silence, Mati frowned. "Okay ... but that's why *we're* here, to rescue them. After all, they don't have starships. They don't even have *rowboats!*"

"True, but what I'm getting at is they don't know *how* to be rescued. They don't understand what's important at a moment like that. They'll always put their old, respected leaders first, and not think of the young females they'll need to start a new civilization."

After pondering Kibi's words in the silence that followed, Rini finally looked at her. "So you mean, we shouldn't let *them* decide who gets in the ship . . ."

"Exactly!"

Mati was frowning again. "That's almost like . . . slavery."

"The alternative is death," Rini pointed out. "And not just for the individuals, but for the whole species, and all their memories and culture."

Mati nodded slightly, but didn't stop frowning.

Sata noticed Boro's mouth hanging open. "What?" she demanded.

"I'm . . . remembering something Ilika once said."

Several people looked at the captain, but he shrugged.

"Manessa," Boro began, "you can put people to sleep, just like our mission bracelets, right?"

"Yes."

"How far away?"

"About one thousand meters."

Boro looked at Kibi with wide eyes, she looked back, and they both nodded.

*

I know they're on the right track, Manessa shared with Arantiloria, *only because I've done simulations like this many times before.*

They're struggling against some powerful instincts. The highly-social creatures have the hardest time with tasks like this because they crave to put social values ahead of physical reality.

The avians can do it, Manessa replied, *after fussing and fuming for a while. You are wise. Do you think these monkey mammals will be able to?*

I don't know. You've known them longer than I have.

The ship was silent.

*

Rini's hand came up timidly.

Kibi looked at him.

"Um . . . I don't think the field's gonna work. The young ones are curious, so they come out of the caves and tunnels first, but then the adults run to the field faster, leaving the young ones confused and following slowly. You see what I'm getting at?"

Kibi frowned.

"That means we have to . . ." Boro began, but didn't finish.

Sata whimpered with pain at the thought.

"That means . . ." Mati started to say, but then had to close her eyes and shudder.

*

Mati claimed a bath tub, hoping it would relax the huge knot in her stomach.

Rini busied himself re-running sensor diagnostics at his station.

Kibi entered the galley and shuffled things around, but didn't accomplish much.

Boro and Sata just held hands in the back of the passenger area.

Ilika smiled to himself, remembering a similar day in his own training.

Suddenly Manessa spoke in her pleasant but urgent voice. "Emergency mission, supernova detected, one sapient race vulnerable, transit time fourteen minutes, complete planetary incineration in twenty-four minutes. Prepare for star transit."

The star drive waited nearly a minute for everyone to get into a meditative state. The crew member in the galley wrestled with several overwhelming emotions before finally getting comfortable and relaxed on the floor.

A moment of eternity later, they could think again.

"Anybody wanna be pilot?" Mati asked as she burst from the bathing room, still pulling on a robe.

No one responded to her offer, so she slid into her seat and began arranging her displays.

"Emergency descent," Kibi ordered, and watched as each crew member did their part. The chart and destination marker quickly appeared, Boro had engines warm almost before Mati spoke, Rini added an infra-red scan, and Ilika declared the ship ready.

The planet's nighttime surface, now mostly glowing cinders, rushed toward them.

"Bunny ears!" the pilot nearly screamed as she slammed her fist onto the special hull configuration symbol.

"Here they come!" the commander squeaked as she felt tears fill her eyes. "Put them to sleep, Manessa!" she shrieked with a broken voice.

Everyone could see the furry white mammals drop to the ground.

"Don't look down, Mati, just land the ship!" Kibi somehow managed to say, heart in her throat.

The pilot was ready. A touch of her display selector switched to three-D topographic, showing her nothing but ground and rocks. She knew she dared not think about anything else. Manessa hit the plaza hard, struts taking most of the shock.

"Hatch open, ramp out!" Ilika declared.

"Seven minutes!" Sata yelled as she started the timer.

"Everybody move!" Kibi screamed. "We've done what we had to do, now let's make something good of it! Two or more at a time!"

✳

They felt nothing, even when they stumbled and scraped arms and legs. All six crew members of the little ship scooped up armloads of furry creatures as fast as they could. Most focused on young females, finding they could carry four or more.

They were all careful to avoid looking at the many furry bodies they had crushed upon landing. Mati was especially careful.

Boro was assigned to get males, larger and far less numerous. He could carry two at a time easily, maybe three, but sometimes he dropped one, and knew he couldn't stop for anything.

Ilika had to activate his bracelet light and enter the cave to find a few older bunnies to provide leadership at their new home. He managed only three trips, two at a time, before he heard Manessa give a twenty-second warning.

Boro was struggling toward the ship with three males when he saw Sata in front of him, her mouth open as if screaming something, but he couldn't hear her. Suddenly she closed her mouth, put her arms across her chest, and tackled him hard. The three limp bunnies went flying. She grabbed his hand, and pulled with all her strength.

For a split second he was confused, then saw everyone else at the hatch, yelling and screaming without sound, so he made his legs move, dove through the hatch with Sata, and a second later it snapped closed behind them.

✳

Boro gasped for breath as he picked himself up from the floor of the entryway, and could see all his shipmates standing or sitting near, all trying to speak to him. But he couldn't hear their words, any of the usual sounds of the ship, or even his own breathing. Eventually he tried to say, "I can't hear anything," but wasn't sure he succeeded.

His shipmates stopped trying to speak to him, so he figured they must have understood him. Sata wrapped her arms around him and laid her head on his chest. Ilika, after looking him over carefully, went up to the passenger area.

Boro could see limp white bunnies all over the floor, several crammed into every seat, four or five on the galley counter, and a few spilling onto the floor of the bridge. As he watched, they all turned into little blue balls of light, then disappeared.

✳

Over the next hour, Boro's hearing slowly returned.

Ilika and Sata, both unhurt, applied ointments and small bandages to scrapes and bruises. Even though Satamia Star Station's medical center was only a short walk away, Ilika explained that it was best to learn all they could from each simulation.

The captain waited until his engineer could hear well enough to share in the good news, then announced the totals. "One hundred and forty-seven young females, eleven young males, and six elders."

"I hope they weren't monogamous," Kibi said with a slight smile.

"They *couldn't* have been," Boro said. "There was only one male to about every twenty females. I really had to hunt to find those eight."

Everyone else laughed, releasing all the tension of a very challenging simulation.

Boro finally sighed. "Can I go to the medical center now, see what happened to my hearing?"

Ilika smiled and nodded. "We'll all go."

✳   ✳   ✳

Chapter 6: Day of Rest

Healer Dakalio couldn't find anything wrong with Boro's ears. He explained that high levels of stress hormones in the human body could cause temporary deafness, and chatted with Boro and Ilika about precautions they should take.

The healer also spent time with Mati, looking for any signs that she was asking too much of her reconstructed knee. K'stimla came in and did the same. Eventually both human and mantis, one with lips and one with mandibles, smiled.

"Whoopee!" Mati cheered.

With the promise of a non-dangerous mission coming up, everyone was in good spirits. After the long training exercise they had just endured, the entire crew of the Manessa Kwi felt they had earned that evening's celebration on Satamia Star Station.

With decorations just starting to go up, Boro and Sata dashed away to spend an hour swimming and fishing with Glorm and his mate.

Kibi and Ilika walked hand-in-hand to the Psychic Development patio, shared a tender kiss by the little bubbling fountain, then entered different chambers to meet with their teachers and get assignments for the up-coming phases of their training. They never knew how long they would be at the star station, as an unexpected mission could interrupt classes, work, or the evening dance party. With a long and easy mission already on their schedule, they both got assignments they could take with them.

Rini noticed that many of Mati's classes had to do with getting fully comfortable with her body, which she had not been able to do at the usual time — childhood. She was not yet attempting the serious dancing that Sata did, nor the extreme tests of courage under pressure that Kibi often endured, but just little things she had missed, like crawling on all fours while talking and playing with others who were working to overcome an injury or handicap of some sort.

At the door to Mati's class, they shared a long embrace, then Rini, not yet in Psychic Development, headed for the Mission Assignment Room.

Rini was in awe of those skilled citizens who worked directly with Kerloran and the heads of the Nebador Services, mortal creatures like himself doing the work of the gods. They had all, he knew, completed Psychic Development and many other programs, so he had simply offered, in a note addressed to Kerloran a few Satamia days before, to be a messenger, sweep the floor, or whatever they needed.

To his surprise, the response had come quickly, asking him to report to someone named Metateron, in the Mission Assignment Room, as soon as he had free time.

As he followed the wide passageway that led to the lowest entrance to the huge spherical room, Rini wondered if Metateron would be bird, reptile, insect, or mammal like himself. The name seemed very strange, so he guessed insect.

The bottom of the Mission Assignment Room, he knew, was a broad circular space that curved upward on all sides. In the center, a pool allowed marine mammals and amphibians to work with avians and other land creatures as critical reports were shared and missions planned. Glowing balls of light, of all possible colors, came and went, while mortals with feet used the three curving ramps that climbed to the many work stations in the massive room.

Rini stood out of the way and wondered how to find Metateron.

A moment later, a fanator floated down from somewhere high above, landed on two feet, and stepped forward. "Rini?"

He nodded. "Are you Metateron?"

The fanator clucked with humor and presented his back for the lad to climb on.

Rini swallowed, as he had only ridden fanators a couple of times, and *this* fanator was not wearing a harness. His mind raced, struggling to remember the short class he had taken that explained where to hold, and where not to.

The giant bird seemed happy with Rini's grip, launched itself into the air with one thrust of its powerful legs, then let its wings take over as the pair began to circle the room and slowly gain altitude.

"Usually you'll have to go up and down the ramps on your own," the fanator said. "This is just for fun, to welcome you to the nerve center of Satamia Star Cluster."

Rini smiled.

✳

Kibi and Ilika emerged from Psychic Development, met at the little fountain as planned, and arrived at the party a little late. They expected to find all their crew members dancing up a storm.

Instead, Rini was on the floor where Mati was busy massaging his sore legs, and both Boro and Sata were nestled in couches, moaning and occasionally scrunching sore shoulders.

Kibi looked down at them and cocked her head.

"We made a mistake," Boro began. "We told Glorm and his lady to swim and fish at their normal pace, and not slow down for us."

"Do you have *any* idea how tirelessly bears can swim?" Sata asked.

Ilika chuckled and grinned. "Some idea."

"And what happened to *you*, Rini?" Kibi asked, sitting on the floor beside Mati.

He turned his head to look at his steward, but stayed on his stomach. "I lost count after a hundred trips up and down the ramps in the Mission Assignment Room, taking knowledge pads here and there, fetching vegetables and seed cakes for people too busy to stop and eat, or just listening to some little meeting Metateron wanted me to hear. I didn't understand much, but I'm starting to get a feel for just how *many things* are going on, all the time, in Satamia."

"My turn!" Mati declared, and lay down on her back.

Rini carefully sat up and began gently massaging her knees.

"Sorest knees in the star station," she explained. "I'm *so* glad I'm not a baby anymore!"

Just then, a lively song began, played by a group of avians, that caused Ilika to start tapping his feet. "Anyone want to dance?"

Four of his crew members just moaned.

"Me!" Kibi said with a grin.

✳   ✳   ✳

Chapter 7: Witnesses

Not long into the following Satamia day, Arantiloria briefed them on their next mission, the one that was supposed to be easy.

Kibi was delighted to discover that it didn't involve any long deep-space trips that would require cramming her cupboards with food.

Boro looked at the flight plan and laughed, saying he could fit *that* much fuel into a pinkfruit juice carton.

The entire crew was excited that an old friend would be among the three passengers.

Ilika decided it was a good mission for some cross training.

✳

"Siminia Three Planet Station, this is response ship Manessa Kwi in low orbit, requesting landing instructions," Rini said from the navigation console.

"Welcome to Siminia, Manessa Kwi!" a male monkey-mammal voice declared in greeting. "No other ship traffic right now, but watch for fanators. Weather is clear, moderate breeze from the west."

A female voice took over. "Use standard approach pattern A, maintain one hundred meters to landing beacon B-One, wait for hand signals, then make visual descent into the indicated landing circle."

Rini touched his console as he listened, then repeated back the instructions.

"Ion three, full inertia canceling," Kibi requested from the pilot's station.

Sata confirmed the engines.

Mati, in the command seat, got a gleam in her eyes. "Visual sensors only."

Boro, at the watch station, moaned and went to work canceling everything else.

Mati turned and smiled at Ilika, currently the steward. "Our passengers won't mind, will they?"

Ilika grinned, then glanced at his passengers.

T'sss'lisss, her coils draped over two seats, shook her head.

Kolarrr'ka fluffed up his feathers. "As I understand it, bok, this mission could takes weeks. A little training won't change that, and might help us with the essays we have to write."

Ashley shrugged. "We're not due back until the Manessa Kwi gets back, and I have no idea what I'm going to write about."

Mati nodded and turned back to the bridge. "Inertia straps."

T'sss'lisss reluctantly coiled herself into one seat.

"Siminia Three Planet Station," Rini began, "our commander has decided to give us a little challenge, so I need some visual landmarks . . ."

*

Nearly an hour later, after navigating by islands, mountain peaks, an old airport gone to weeds, and finally the giant artificial tree in the center of the planet station, the Manessa Kwi hovered over a landing circle where a monkey mammal stood with his arms out-stretched, a bright-red marker light in each hand.

Kibi knew the landing circle could hold much larger ships, so wasn't surprised when the landing controller swung his arms for the little ship to follow. He soon stopped in the middle of a smaller circle, turned completely around with arms wide, then shut off his marker lights and moved out of the way.

Kibi lowered the deep-space response ship, extended struts, and carefully brought her power levels to zero. "Finished with engines."

As the passengers and crew came down the ramp, they beheld two tall, proud monkey mammals, most of their bodies covered with fur, long tails swaying in the air behind them.

But as the new arrivals approached, the pair seemed to shrink, became hunched with age, leaned on each other, and everyone could see that their fur was gray, almost white, and in places very thin.

The female began coughing, and the male comforted her. They hobbled toward a bench in the shade of a building. A large avian and an ursine with a medical kit, who had both stayed out of sight before, walked with them.

Once they got settled, the elderly male monkey mammal looked at the bird. "Thanks, Rrr'tana, for letting us do that one last time. It's been years, and it was great fun."

Rrr'tana bowed with sad eyes.

The bear kept two eyes on her charges, but said nothing.

Kibi knelt on the ground in front of the bench, and the other crew members and passengers did the same. T'sss'lisss was already on the ground.

The ancient female monkey mammal tried to clear her throat, without complete success. "Thank you for coming. You are witnesses, as we once were. You will hear our story, if we are blessed with enough time to tell it." She started coughing again, and quickly mastered it, but didn't have the energy to go on speaking, so she looked at her partner.

"I am Jimox, and this is Teina. We have been the hosts of Siminia Three

Planet Station for . . . how long?"

Teina searched her memory. "Just had the two-hundred-year celebration last year . . ."

Jimox scrunched his wrinkled face. "Wasn't that three or four years ago?"

"Maybe. I don't remember."

Jimox kissed her tenderly, then turned back to his guests. "Let's just say . . . a long time!"

Everyone chuckled.

"Of course," he went on, "we don't do any of the work anymore. We poke around, talk to people a little, but someone else has to finish anything we start. Rrr'tana, and others, are the *real* hosts now. Brora is a wonderful healer, but there isn't much she can do for us anymore. Somehow, in between all the things we've done in our lives, we got old."

Among the listeners, not all eyes were dry. Teina looked ready to speak, so Jimox deferred to her.

"We have hundreds of friends we know by name, and thousands more we remember, but . . . we didn't want . . . a big fuss . . ." Nearly blue from the effort of speaking, she looked at Jimox.

"We want this to be a quiet time, and Kerloran wants us to have a few witnesses with a fresh perspective on our lives and our work, so . . . we decided to invite people who've never been here before. It was hard to find anyone . . ."

Several people chuckled. T'sss'lisss' coils quivered with humor.

". . . so I'm not surprised that all of you are young. Manessa has been here before, but with a different crew, avians as I remember."

Ilika smiled.

"We need to tell them!" Teina managed to whisper.

"I know. You want to?"

"I . . . don't have the strength."

Jimox turned back to the guests. "Kerloran tells us we have four great missions. Three of them we know all about, and have completed to the best of our abilities. The fourth one . . . we don't know much about yet. You are here because . . . we are dying."

✳   ✳   ✳

Chapter 8: No Longer Alone

Having said that much, the two elderly monkey mammals slumped onto the bench with exhaustion, and their healer insisted they take a break for food and medicine.

The crew of the Manessa Kwi, and the three Education Service trainees, poked around that part of the planet station, soon discovering a small artificial lake with tiny rowboats for anyone who wanted to explore the nearby woods and islands by water. Two reptiles in one boat, and an ursine in another, were having a friendly race. The ursine was winning.

The crew was tempted to try the little water craft, but Jimox and Teina were soon back, eager to begin their story.

✳ ✳ ✳

Wet snow and freezing rain had been falling for two weeks, but never quite sticking. Finally, a day dawned when everything seemed willing to stay up in the clouds.

Jimox emerged from his soggy tent early, anxious to get out and do something. That camp was almost out of food, so he stretched his brown furry arms, shouldered a large backpack and his bow and quiver, and headed south into the suburbs where he knew scrounging would be good.

By mid-day, his pack was bulging with food, and only one arrow was missing from his quiver. The dog had mis-judged the abilities of his intended victim, but had broken the arrow in its death throws. Jimox had salvaged the razor-sharp broadhead and stiff turkey feathers to fit to a new shaft someday.

Now the young monkey mammal was heading home, taking a shortcut through a neighborhood he hadn't explored before. Most of the houses were burned, like everywhere else, but a small children's school was intact, though very overgrown with weeds.

Jimox glanced up at the street sign as he crossed a small intersection. Twenty-Seventh Street didn't go much of anywhere in either direction, but he knew he could turn right at Thirtieth Street and be less than a mile from one of his camps. A sea gull squawked from a chimney whose house had burned down around it. Jimox thought he saw a ghost hovering near the chimney, as if tending a fire, but couldn't be sure in the daylight. He shifted the weight on his shoulders and trudged on.

Soon after crossing Twenty-Eighth Street, his heavy pack was causing his back muscles to scream at him, so he looked around. A low stone wall called to him, with a good view in all directions. The house above had burned, though an old detached garage, with a peaked roof, was still standing.

He turned a complete circle, scanning and listening for dog sounds, or any other signs of danger, then rested his pack on the stone wall and slipped out of the straps. A deep sigh escaped him as his back and shoulders regained their freedom.

He opened his backpack. The package of crackers and peanut butter were a little stale, but not yet rancid, so he chewed, knowing they would nourish him and he could wash them down with a carton of apple juice.

"Hi," came a soft voice from behind him.

Within seconds, he had grabbed his bow, fitted an arrow, and was spinning around even as he began to pull back the string.

The girl standing there, not far from the garage, was only seven or eight, but in response to his bow and arrow, she flashed out a hunting knife about a foot long.

Jimox relaxed his string and lowered the bow to his side. "Hi."

She lowered her knife. "Are you . . . real?"

"Yep. Not a ghost . . . yet."

"And no . . . disease?"

"Nope. You?"

She slipped her knife back into its sheath on her belt. "I thought I was the only one."

"Me too. I haven't seen another person alive since . . . middle of last summer. Wanna . . . share some crackers, apple juice, maybe a candy bar?"

"Um . . . sure."

✳

Teina was seven, four years younger than Jimox. She had run into a patch of woods, the previous summer, when her parents started burning down their house, and had stayed there, peeking out with wide eyes as her world burned around her.

Sometimes the smoke nearly drove her out, but she could see nowhere better to go. Eventually she emerged to find herself completely alone, save for a few diseased and dying people dragging themselves around town looking for something to eat, or more often, just something to burn.

She had coughed for weeks, as she picked through the ruins and hardened herself to the circumstances of her new life. She quickly noticed that the dying people were all drawn to their houses, or someone else's house if they had none, and were completely ignoring the shops and stores. She worked all day, every day, to protect food and other supplies from the mice and rats that were beginning to creep everywhere, and the birds who would get in through any broken window.

Jimox shared a similar experience. He had been camping in the back yard when his parents began to feel the effects of the disease. Luckily, he now realized, the house was completely in flames before he could get back inside to see what was going on. The heat quickly forced him down to the little creek at the bottom of the yard.

By chance, he had focused his scrounging efforts, in the weeks and months that followed, in a different part of town. He opened his map, and they both laughed when they saw that Teina's territory was close to, but perfectly separate from Jimox' territory, almost as if someone had drawn boundaries. Only his short cut, that day, had caused their paths to cross.

Suddenly Teina froze, listening.

Jimox instinctively grabbed his bow.

"Too many! Follow me!" she asserted.

He took his bow and quiver in one hand, his pack by one strap, and dashed up the stone steps behind Teina, hearing the sounds of a pack of dogs rapidly approaching.

She ran behind the garage and scampered up a ladder.

He paused at the bottom, tossed his bow and quiver up to her, then shouldered his pack. Three or four large dogs rounded the corner of the building.

He set boots to the ladder, but canine teeth began tearing at his pants. He struggled to ascend each rung. One dog fell off as Jimox shook his leg. Another could only be dislodged by kicking its head with his opposite boot. The third, the largest of the pack, leapt halfway up the ladder and sank its teeth into Jimox' leg, but a moment later released its grip and dropped to the ground, a feathered shaft piercing its side.

The boy's leg throbbed and burned with pain, but he climbed, got onto the sloping woodshed roof, tossed off his pack, and collapsed onto the shingles.

"Get your pants off!" Teina commanded. "I'll get my first aid stuff." She disappeared into a window of the attic above the garage.

Jimox was nearly as stunned by her assertive manner as by the pain in his leg. He was used to girls, especially seven-year-olds, having few abilities other than dressing their dolls.

But while he wondered about her, he did what she ordered, knowing well the condition of his leg would determine whether he lived or died. He forced himself to think, and realized the bone must not be broken, as he had been able, moments before, to finish climbing the ladder.

He got his pants off about when Teina returned with a big first-aid box.

Jimox looked at his leg, not daring to touch it. "The teeth didn't get through my pants, but I'm gonna have lots of scabs, and one hell of a bruise. Antiseptic?"

"Can you stand alcohol?"

He shuddered at the thought, but knew it would do the best job. "Do it."

She reached into her box, unscrewed the cap, and poured.

He screamed, and tears of pain flowed down his face.

"Sorry," she mumbled, and kept pouring.

✳

An hour later, his pants and socks had been sterilized with alcohol and were drying while Jimox munched cookies and listened to Teina share her experiences. More than once during the last ten months, she had to bravely doctor herself after brushes with rusty nails, broken glass, or hungry rats.

Jimox tested his leg, and could slowly walk around on the woodshed roof, but judged that he would have great trouble getting to any of his camps, the nearest about a mile away.

Teina swallowed once. "If you and me are partners, then you have another camp, right here."

Jimox took a minute to remember the state of the world in which he lived.

Eventually he sensed the importance of the moment, made eye contact with Teina, and nodded.

*

Her home was the attic space above an old garage, with windows in the front and back under the peaks of the roof. Luckily, the garage had not housed a car, or anything else dangerous or smelly. Boards she found in many different places had finished the floor, then made shelves, now stocked with every manner of food and supplies.

Jimox opened his map again, and shared the locations of his seven camps, promising to give her the grand tour as soon as his leg was better.

Not much later, the sun found the western horizon, somewhere above the thick winter clouds, and the pair of young monkey mammals lit a candle and prepared a simple dinner.

They had both endured ten months alone, eight of those without seeing another living person. Neither had any idea why the plague had spared them, and as far as they could tell, no one else. No purpose or task gave their lives meaning, other than to sift through the ruins and save anything that looked edible or useful.

But that evening, eating canned food by candlelight, their hearts sang with joy, knowing they would no longer be alone.

*   *   *

"For many years after that, Teina and I never went more than about a hundred meters from each other," Jimox shared. "Neither one of us ever wanted to be alone again. We cooked together, explored new places together, and scrounged for food and supplies together, but we didn't sleep right together."

"At first we were too young to be interested," Teina explained. "Then we were afraid of me getting pregnant with no healers or working hospitals *anywhere.*"

Jimox smiled, his gaze lost in fond memories.

*   *   *

Chapter 9: Raison d'être

"For years we struggled to imagine what our purpose might be," Jimox shared. "Why would two monkey mammals survive, when everyone else died, unless it was for some reason?"

"We had a purpose," Teina continued the thought, "and we actually started fulfilling it about a week after the plague, but we just didn't know it for *years*."

"Let's see ..." Jimox thought back, "six years at home, almost a year traveling, then five more here."

"We'll show you!" she said, and started to hop up, but suddenly cried out in pain and fell back down.

Jimox quickly comforted her with arms and soft words. "The same pain?"

Teina nodded while trembling.

"Should we call for a team of healers from Satamia?" Kibi asked anxiously, finger poised over her mission bracelet.

Without looking up from his beloved partner, Jimox answered. "They know all about it, and there's nothing they can do. We know how to manage it, but sometimes we forget and think we're young again. Brora will be back from rounds any minute now, and has some medicine that helps a little."

Teina whimpered through her pain. "I'll be okay in a moment."

Several minutes later, with Jimox' help, Teina carefully stood up, but Kibi could still see pain in her eyes. The pair of original planet station hosts slowly led the crew of the Manessa Kwi to a part of the station called Olde Towne, full of quaint buildings from a time past.

Soon they came to one that had been a large restaurant. It now contained display cases of many shapes and sizes, paintings on the walls, sculptures on pedestals, book shelves where nothing else would fit, and display screens facing a bench or two. In several places, pairs or trios of visitors watched a video or examined the works on display.

"This museum contains the most important art works and books from our civilization," Jimox explained. "We think it's silly, but the curators insisted that our journals go in here."

They approached a display case with several books held open to pages of children's drawings or simple writing. A bird and a large insect sat side by side on a nearby bench, studying pages from these or similar books on a display screen, taking notes as they worked.

"When the plague happened, I didn't even know how to write!" Teina admitted after Jimox helped her onto a bench. "I was only six. But as I scrounged through stores for food and supplies, I always grabbed blank writing and drawing books. I didn't really know why, I just couldn't help myself."

Jimox smiled. "I was doing the same thing in another part of town."

"Jimox taught me to write, but at first I just drew pictures of what was happening — sun shining, weeds growing, burned houses smoldering, dogs eating dead people, you know, the usual stuff."

Rini grinned at her.

"I *barely* knew how to write, just stick letters and lots of misspelling," Jimox added. "But years later, we studied our early journals, and they really helped us to piece together what happened, and when. We figured out when the last other person died from a drawing of a dark rain cloud in Teina's journal, and 'RAIND AL DA' in mine." He spelled the words for his guests, and they laughed.

Teina laughed too, then started coughing deeply. Kibi rubbed her back until she recovered. "That was . . . that was in the middle of summer, we lived way up north. It's a retreat now, and people from all over Nebador go there to peek in the window of our old attic over the garage. It's embarrassing."

Jimox smiled. "So before the smoke had even cleared, many months before we met, we were busy fulfilling our first, and probably most important, mission. We were alive because the universe needed witnesses to what our civilization had done to itself. We later found out we couldn't have children because a species that does very stupid things has no business continuing into the future. But the memory of our people, who were *way* too full of themselves, needed to be preserved so that others could learn from their mistakes."

T'sss'lisss laid her head on Teina's lap. "I hope I have asss much wisssdom and experienccce asss you sssomeday."

Teina stroked the smooth scales, front to back. "You will, and probably much more. On Satamia Star Station, you get to walk and talk with the gods every day. They only visit us here . . . maybe . . . once or twice a week."

✳ ✳ ✳

Seven-year-old Teina colored in a gray cloud above the warehouse they had just explored. She noticed Jimox peeking over her shoulder, and spoke while coloring. "Warehouses never seem to be very good scrounging."

"I know, but it was nice to do something out of the rain. I felt sorry for the two ghosts carrying boxes back and forth. Want to share journals from the first summer, just after Burning Day?"

A shadow passed over Teina. "What good will *that* do?"

"One of us might have noticed something the other didn't, something that will help us understand what happened."

"But *my* journals are just silly little drawings. Yours are much better 'cause *you* know how to write."

Jimox considered for a moment. "I was thinking that mine are ugly and boring, and yours are beautiful with all the colors and feelings you put into them."

After a moment, Teina cracked a tiny smile. "Okay."

They each had a private shelf, on their own side of the garage attic, by their beds. From these came their earliest journals, almost a year old.

"Here's a man who ran into the woods where I was hiding," she explained.

Jimox gazed at the simple drawing of a person with the plague, hair and eyes wild, arms and tail waving in the air.

"He tried to light a fire, but everything was too green. Luckily, he didn't see me."

"Did you draw your parents?"

"No. And I'm not gonna."

Jimox nodded. "I wrote about mine, but it took months to work up the courage. I was so mad at them . . . but it wasn't like they *chose* to get the plague."

"I know what you mean. I remember the wild, crazy look in their eyes, and it wasn't really them, the parents I used to have. They looked more like . . . the sick man in the woods."

* * *

"We discovered little things each of us had missed, but mostly it was good therapy for us," Jimox explained.

"About a year later, I even drew my parents!" Teina revealed, but the effort brought on a fit of coughing.

After she recovered, Jimox struggled to share something that obviously was very difficult for him. "It wasn't until . . . years later, in the big city to the north, that we . . . discovered the truth."

Teina closed her eyes.

"All the terrible things that people did when they got the plague," Jimox said slowly with a heavy heart, "it was all by design. The plague wasn't some natural disease that got loose from a lab that was studying it. It was . . ." He had to stop and swallow several times. "It was *planned* to work that way . . . by our leaders . . . from the very beginning of the project . . ."

* * *

Chapter 10: Listening Lessons

"The most horrible part of my life was followed by the most wonderful part," Teina explained, but had no more strength for speaking, so she looked at Jimox.

Jimox turned to the many faces gathered around, more than twenty now, eager to hear the story even if they had heard it before. "What Teina said was true, but we wouldn't have been ready for that wonderful part without the horrible year that came before."

Teina nodded.

"At ages seven and eleven . . . seven and thirteen in Nebador numbers . . . most kids on our planet wouldn't have been ready for a working relationship like we had to quickly develop . . ."

✳   ✳   ✳

While Teina finished boiling water on a little camp stove, Jimox worked on highlighting areas on a map. She stirred in instant cereal and handed him a bowl and spoon.

"Thanks. I've finished marking my picked-clean places in orange, and my lightly-picked areas in yellow."

"Good. I want to start scrounging in that neighborhood just south of the motorway. It's the closest one I haven't cleaned out, and you haven't touched it."

Jimox looked thoughtful as he ate his cereal and gazed at the map. "Are you thinking we should bring everything here?"

Teina appeared slightly bothered by his question. "Yeah, or to one of your camps."

After scraping out his bowl, Jimox unfolded another map that showed a larger area, and all the main roads, but not every little street. "I have an idea to share. After I share it, I'll let you decide, okay?"

She shrugged.

"Scrounging close to our house and camps will get the most stuff stacked up in those places. But while we're slowly picking one or two cans of food out of each ruin, rats are eating through all the paper and plastic packages in all the grocery stores in ... these suburbs farther out ... and all these small towns out in the country."

"But they're so far!" Teina began with a tone of frustration. "Even if we used bicycles, we'd be riding all day just for one little load!"

Jimox let a long moment pass before continuing. "True. But what will happen when we've picked clean *all* the areas close to our house and camps?"

Teina looked back with wide eyes. "I don't know."

"Remember, I'm just asking you to listen to my idea."

She took several deep breaths to collect herself.

"I suggest that wherever there are stores and restaurants, and sometimes unburned houses with good scrounging, we go there and protect as much stuff as possible, as quickly as possible, from rats, birds, insects ... you know the list."

She forced out a smile. "Yep!"

"And we just leave it there. If we need it someday, *we* can go to *it*. We can spend days, even weeks, riding between suburbs and little towns, spending however long we want in each place, setting up a safe house, protecting the food, then moving on. When we feel ready to come back here, we can bring a load. That's my idea. Your choice."

* * *

"It took me *days* to get my head around Jimox' idea," Teina shared with her listeners. "I was only seven years old, and he was challenging me to think about a strategy that would maximize our food supply in the long-term, while I was thinking like a little squirrel, just wanting to pull as many nuts as possible into my nest in the short-term." She paused to cough. "He never asked again. We even went scrounging close-by several times. Then I started dreaming about rats and bugs eating the food we *could* be saving."

Many of her listeners chuckled.

"The next morning, as soon as he poked his head out of his sleeping bag, I looked at him and said, 'You're right. Let's get bikes and start saving stuff.'"

"For the next three years," Jimox took up the story, "we journeyed in wider and wider circles, eventually exploring the big cities north and south of our home town. There are still food stashes in a hundred places up there, maybe some of it still good today."

Teina made a face and shook her head.

Jimox grinned. "And we had to learn to listen to each other in many different situations . . ."

* * *

The two young monkey mammals, now wearing gun belts and holsters, crept into the sporting goods store through an upstairs apartment and office. The apartment had given them a few cans of tuna, but their primary mission was the large rack of freeze-dried food they could see through the front window, and maybe some propane camp-stove bottles.

Jimox led the way along the narrow inside balcony toward the spiral staircase. Suddenly Teina touched his arm. "Stop, I sense danger!"

Jimox looked down, but didn't see anything. "I can handle it," he asserted, patting his new holster and the pistol inside. "Wait here while I scout."

Teina breathed a silent sigh as Jimox descended the metal stair. It creaked under his weight.

He reached the bottom and started to walk around on the main floor of the store when he smelled something, but didn't have time to think before two large dogs came bolting out of the storeroom in the back.

Jimox tried to pull out his pistol, but dropped it, judged he didn't have time to pick it up, ran, and hopped onto a table, scattering sun hats and dark glasses in all directions.

The growling, snapping dogs each took one side of the table, just barely big enough to protect Jimox from their hungry jaws if he stood in the very middle. He could see his pistol on the floor. He looked up and saw Teina leaning on the balcony rail. "Help!" he called.

"Why?" Teina asked. "I tried to warn you. You wouldn't listen."

Jimox tried kicking at the dogs, but they were quick and avoided his boots. "It looked safe!"

"But you forgot about smell, and all the things in the store that are chewed up, and plain old gut instincts. And even if *your* instincts weren't working, *mine* were!"

"I will never, ever again ignore your warnings, I promise!"

"And you thought your new gun could handle *anything*."

"I was wrong!" Jimox admitted, almost dancing to keep away from the canine teeth on both sides of him. "It's too easy to fumble it when something's running at you."

Teina took a slow, deep breath. "Boys," she mumbled to herself, pulled out her pistol, and took careful aim.

One dog squealed, ran a few feet, and dropped. The other barked with anger and grief as it ran back toward the storeroom.

"I think you should stay on the table until I get down there to cover you," Teina said, starting down the spiral staircase.

Jimox, feeling about an inch tall, did as she said.

✳ ✳ ✳

Chapter 11: The Thinking Place

A clear, breezy summer day beckoned the pair out into the sunshine. They had just returned from a week-long scrounging trip to several smaller towns, and their shelves were well-stocked, so they just grabbed sun hats and day packs. As they neared the middle of town, sea gulls seemed to call them out onto the docks where big ships once unloaded their cargos, but which now stood empty.

Teina was unusually quiet, glancing at warehouses, but feeling no temptation to explore them.

Jimox noticed a lunch counter they hadn't searched, but decided to go with Teina's mood. He knew that scrounging in other towns, and leaving most of the goodies there, was not her first choice, but she was doing it because it needed to be done. Today, he would follow her lead. They could peek at the lunch counter on the way back if they felt like it.

On the big deep-water dock, the two huge cargo cranes, silhouetted against a light-blue sky, creaked slightly as the two little monkey mammals passed beneath their shadows. A massive cold-storage building sat nearby, but they had already agreed to never even open the door, considering what would be growing inside after more than a year without electricity.

Beyond the dock and warehouse area, they came to a fence. Where the road ran through, a sign said *Harbor Master — Official Business Only*. Several plain gray buildings clustered at the very end of the road. One bristled with weather instruments and a radar antenna, no longer turning. Another was about twenty feet up on stilts.

"I've never been out here," Jimox admitted.

"Me neither."

They both smiled slightly as they passed the *Official Business Only* sign.

"Kind of fun to be able to ignore all the rules," Teina said.

Jimox nodded. "One of the few advantages of being the only people alive."

Teina chuckled as they walked toward the building on stilts.

✳

The little gate across the stairway piqued their interest. Meant to keep out people without a key, it had little chance against two determined kids with bolt cutters, but was still able to do its job against dogs.

Even so, Teina ascended the steps with pistol drawn.

At the top, sea gulls completely owned the outside balcony, with nests and droppings everywhere. They shrieked at the intruders, but gave way when Jimox waved his arms.

After walking all the way around the building, both monkey mammals pressed their faces to the dusty glass. They beheld one large room with tables and chairs, couches, a little kitchen, and several electrical devices with glowing lights.

"Electricity?" Teina wondered aloud with wide eyes.

Jimox' face suddenly lit up. He dashed back to a section of balcony without windows, then climbed a little ladder up to the roof. "Yep. There's a solar panel up here," he reported as he climbed back down.

Teina tried the door, and discovered it wasn't locked. "They must have figured the gate at the bottom was enough."

✳

Without discussion, they went to work making it theirs. The only ghost stayed near a telescope in one corner and ignored them. Out of respect, they didn't touch the telescope.

The working electrical devices were radios, Jimox found, with every possible chart and reference book handy.

Teina checked the little toilet room, and found a rack of four big batteries. No water ran in the plumbing, but bottled water and paper towels allowed them to give the place a good cleaning.

They knew not to open the little refrigerator, as it wasn't part of the solar-power system.

Eventually they settled onto a couch, and could see the entire bay, sparkling in the afternoon light, spread out before them. Both young survivors fell silent, and their earlier thoughtful mood returned.

*

"You said something on the way here," Teina began after watching sea gulls walk around on the balcony railing for a few minutes. "I haven't been able to get it out of my head. You said we were the only people alive. That made me remember how you and me were practically *neighbors* for most of a year, but never knew about each other. How can we *ever* know if we're the only people alive?"

Jimox pondered her question for a long minute. "You're right, we can't." He thought about it further. "If a large group of people was living somewhere, they'd change things enough to give themselves away. You know, heavy scrounging, fixing up buildings, burning things to stay warm, growing gardens . . ."

"Or a small group that was really noisy and careless," she added.

"Yeah. But a small, careful group, or a single person, could stay hidden for a *long* time. We'd have to scrounge in the same places to see the signs."

Teina thought for a minute. "In all our scrounging, or yours before we met, have you *ever* seen anything that made you think someone else was alive?"

He considered her question carefully. "After the middle of last summer . . . and not counting things animals did . . . no."

After several slow breaths, she said, "Me neither."

*

Jimox carried the little refrigerator outside and Teina opened it with a broom handle. They saw the puff of green mold spores, and quickly ran back inside and closed the door.

Jimox tried the radios. They seemed to be in working order, but he could find nothing but the hiss of natural background static.

Teina pulled some snacks out of her day pack, and they returned to the couch.

"I think I see the answer to your question," he said after chewing a fruit bar. "At least . . . the only answer I can give you."

She looked at him with anticipation.

"We can never search the whole world for people. Even if we spent our entire *lives* doing it, we could walk right by a house where someone was hiding. But we can watch the harbor for ships, like from here. We can watch the sky for airplanes. Nothing can take-off or land at this airport without being visible from our house and some of the camps. We can use battery radios, like here, to see if anyone is transmitting *anything*."

Teina nodded. "And we can do all that in the big cities too."

"Right. We can watch the motorways and the train tracks, maybe stretch threads across like they do in spy movies so we'll know if anything came by while we weren't looking . . ."

Teina chuckled.

"We can probably do other things I haven't thought of yet. We'll get a pretty good idea of what's going on in the world, even though we can never know for sure."

Teina nodded with understanding, but didn't otherwise respond. After a minute, she got cleaning supplies and went outside to tackle the little refrigerator.

Jimox hadn't expected a response. He grabbed a trash bag and went out to help.

✳ ✳ ✳

"That was the biggest question that haunted us in those early years," Teina shared, "but there were others, and that harbor control tower became our thinking place."

Jimox slowly nodded. "The next biggest question, for me, was exactly what happened to cause the plague. Even as kids, we knew that the people were never told the whole story about stuff like that."

"That made us start searching . . ." She paused to catch her breath. ". . . through mayors' and governors' offices whenever we went to the big cities."

Jimox nodded. "Fire chief, police chief, emergency services, any place they might know the *real* story."

"And we started making more rules," Teina added, "about what we'd do if we ever found someone alive."

Jimox smiled. "By then I had learned to listen to Teina, even though she *was* just a girl."

They grinned at each other, and all the listeners laughed.

"Actually, it was pretty easy," Jimox went on, "because the truth is, she's a lot smarter than me in things that really matter . . ."

Teina snuggled close and hide her embarrassment in Jimox' gray fur.

"Maybe I could do technical stuff, but she could imagine situations in which we'd have an eighth of a second to make a life-or-death decision, *our* life or death!"

Teina suddenly raised her head. "But none of our rules did us much good when the Nebador ship arrived."

✳ ✳ ✳

Chapter 12: Leaving Home

"Almost six years had passed since the plague — five since Teina and I met — when we realized we were ready for a change."

"We weren't little kids anymore," Teina asserted. "I was twelve . . . I mean fourteen. Older people on this planet, when there still were any, would have *called* me a little kid, but my short childhood was far in the past, and barely remembered."

Jimox nodded. "We had safe houses and food stashes in twenty or more little towns, and several in the big cities to the north and south. A military base to the east had given us a warehouse full of dry canned food that was supposed to last forever. As best we could figure, we had enough for the rest of our lives."

Kibi smiled at the thought.

"We knew as much about the plague as any public official had ever been told," Teina took up the story. "We had watched the harbors, airports, motorways, and train tracks for two hundred miles up and down the coast, and from the ocean to the mountains." She paused to find her voice again. "We had listened to every radio frequency, at different times, on different days. Except for the wild creatures, we were as alone as any two monkey mammals could be."

"It was early spring," Jimox said, searching his memory, "and the winter had been *really* cold . . ."

*   *   *

Teina, dressed warmly and with a blanket over her shoulders, huddled by the propane heater as she wrote in her journal.

Jimox peeked out from under the covers. "Good morning."

"Hi. I was so tired last night when we got in that I forgot to write."

"Me too. I'll make breakfast, *then* I'll write. I think . . . potato patties and scrambled eggs."

Teina concentrated on her journal while Jimox worked with instant potatoes, powdered eggs, and spices. Finally she closed her journal book and started helping with breakfast. "I know I was the one who was always dragging my feet about exploring other towns and cities," she began, "but now, every time I look at the map, I catch myself wondering about ... that big city way down south ..." She unfolded a map to refresh her memory. "Westron."

Jimox laughed as he turned patties in the frying pan. "You mean ... where it's warmer?"

She smiled as she stirred powdered milk into cups of water. "It seems like we spend three-quarters of the year shivering, especially the last couple of years."

"Why don't we go?" he posed as he slipped potato patties onto plates, then poured eggs into the frying pan.

Teina's eyes grew wide. "You mean, just go?"

While the eggs cooked, they dove into their potato patties. Jimox spoke between bites. "After picking out the best bikes, getting spare parts, securing stuff here ... you know."

Teina's brow remained wrinkled as she thought about it.

Jimox served hot, spicy scrambled eggs.

It snowed that day, and Teina was glad. It gave them lots of time to look at maps, think, and talk.

Mid-afternoon had passed when she finally blurted out the concern that was driving her crazy. "We just spent six years of our lives scraping up food and stuff! How can we take it with us?"

Jimox let a moment pass before answering. "We can't." After saying that, he could have sworn he saw smoke coming out of Teina's ears.

"But we can't just leave it all here!"

"Why not? We'll find more along the way, and we'll always know there's a lifetime of supplies here if we ever need them."

Teina wasn't ready to say anything else, so she looked at the map again.

*

For several days, in between necessary trips out into the cold, they pondered the journey they both craved and dreaded to make, each for different reasons.

Jimox shared his fears of huge dog packs overwhelming their firepower, even with each of them carrying several pistols. He admitted that he'd kept his eyes open for machine guns in the stores, but hadn't seen any.

Teina smiled, and reminded him that any time more than about six dogs got together, a fight broke out that kept the packs small. But somehow, listening to his fears helped her put her own into perspective.

They gazed at the maps for hours, and both frowned at the steep mountain passes, and the desert roads with long stretches between towns. That left the winding coastal route.

They made calculations, based on the distances they liked to pedal closer to home, added days for scrounging, and realized it would be a journey of four to six months.

Jimox suddenly grinned. "Perfect! We can leave here in the summer, when it's nicest, and by the time we get down there, it'll be winter, when it's nicest. We won't freeze or bake! Shall we do it?"

Teina looked at him, and realized she could definitely take one thing with her on this journey, and every journey — the thing in her life that mattered most. "Yeah!"

* * *

"We both suddenly felt the irresistible urge to check all our safe houses and food stashes," Jimox shared with a grin.

Teina chuckled, coughed for a moment, then smiled. "That took half the summer!"

"And we were both *very* picky about what we took with us, changing our minds almost daily."

"That was mostly me, and took another month," Teina admitted.

"The hardest thing to leave behind was our journals."

Teina nodded.

"There were just too many of them! We could take them, or a little food, but not both."

Everyone laughed.

"Food won," Teina said with a smile.

"But those old journals were lovingly wrapped up in plastic bags, then locked in sturdy metal boxes!"

"Little did we know . . ." Teina paused to clear her throat. "Little did we know we'd be coming back to get them, about seven years later, in a Nebador life-monitor ship."

All the listeners clucked, smiled, or shook their scales.

* * *

After two days of pedaling, then crossing a bridge over the mouth of a river, the pair of young travelers came to the first town they had never set foot in before. They coasted to a stop while still in open country, two or three blocks from the buildings.

"*Now* I feel like the journey has begun," Jimox declared as he pulled out a spyglass.

Teina swiveled in her seat to watch sides and rear.

"Grocery store looks intact," Jimox reported. "A mangy mutt poking around. One motel burned down. Taco stand. I can't see much more."

"Those same five or six ghosts are still following us," Teina remarked. "One more than yesterday, I think."

"I wonder why they ignored us for five years, and all of a sudden we're super-interesting."

Teina shrugged. "We didn't exactly keep it a secret that we were leaving, maybe for a long time."

"True. I thought they'd be glad to get rid of us. Little motel on the left, just before the grocery store, looks like the best bet. It's definitely a one-mutt town."

Teina laughed and checked her pistol.

✻ ✻ ✻

"So we began riding from town to town, and they were all about the same," Jimox shared, searching his memory. "We soon knew we could handle it. Dogs were few, and usually weak from hunger. Most houses had burned, like everywhere else, but there was always *something* we could camp in. Scrounging was good in most places, and we always carried food for an unlucky day or two."

Teina jumped in. "But for weeks, we couldn't figure out why ghosts were following us, more and more of them all the time."

"Then we came to Gibson's Bay, where we learned more about ghosts than we *ever* wanted to know."

✳   ✳   ✳

Chapter 13: Spookville

A gentle breeze and overcast sky kept Jimox and Teina cool as they pedaled hard, in low gear. They crested a rise and saw the small sea-side town below, an idyllic little fishing and tourist village, complete with clam chowder restaurant on the pier, gulls calling to each other, and waves splashing on the rocks below.

They coasted to a stop at the high-point of the road, planted their shoes on the warm pavement, and linked tails for courage. A sign beside the road said *Welcome To*, but the rest had been ripped away by some winter storm.

"Population four hundred and twenty-nine," Jimox mumbled. "More ghosts to add to the thirty or so on our tail."

Teina chuckled as she pulled a little spyglass from her handle-bar bag. Jimox kept watch to the rear and sides, and while doing so, made sure his pistol was fully loaded.

"A small grocery store on the street . . ." she began, "sporting goods store across from it . . . restaurant on the pier is all smashed up . . . a little sandwich shop, I think, on the street . . . the usual burned-down houses . . . not much else." She lowered the spyglass.

"Movement?"

"Just gulls. See what you can see."

He took the spyglass and scanned the town. "I guess that pile of sticks was a boat marina once."

"You could have fooled me."

He snickered and continued scanning. "Dog! On the beach beyond the pier."

"I see it," she said, shielding her eyes from the bright clouds.

"Small and scrawny, shouldn't give us much trouble. Appears to be alone."

"Eating dead sea gulls."

Jimox lowered the spyglass. "That's what's on the menu in *this* little town."

✳

A gift shop not far from the pier looked clean and dry inside, so Jimox got out his pry bar while Teina stood with her feet wide apart, facing the street and fingering the cylinder of her small revolver. A sea gull squawked at her from a lamp post that had been dark for more than five years. When she heard the snap of breaking metal behind her, she listened as Jimox opened the door, but kept her attention on the street.

"Clear and clean in the main shop," he announced. "Okay, bikes are in."

Teina backed in, letting the heavy glass door close behind her. "Self-closing and only opens outward ... my favorite kind. Sorry, doggy. Monkey mammal is *not* on the menu today."

Jimox used about a minute of their precious flashlight battery power to light every corner of the storeroom in back while Teina followed with gun drawn. From the good condition of the shop, and the absence of odor, they doubted anything lurked within, but knew they wouldn't sleep until they were sure.

At least, nothing mortal lurked within.

As they unrolled sleeping bags, both caught glimpses of tiny shimmering lights or dark shadows in the corners and near the ceiling of the shop.

"Three or four resident ghosts, just curious so far," Teina shared.

Jimox looked around. "I sense a tinge of anger."

Teina nodded. "Scout the town? We've got plenty of daylight."

"Yeah! Maybe something tasty for dinner ..."

✳

Over the next two hours, the travelers sampled all the services the little town had to offer. The chowder restaurant was just a ruin, and the grocery store had been fouled and picked clean by birds entering through a broken window. The sandwich shop, however, appeared to be intact, so they propped open doors to air out the stench while they checked the rest of the buildings.

A growing troop of little shadows followed them, more felt than seen while the sun was up.

"Someone's angry," Teina said after shivering from the tingly feeling on the back of her neck. "More than we had following us this morning."

"That's what I was thinking. They must have called for reinforcements."

She laughed while rubbing the dust off a window. "Just an office. No candy machine or anything."

"The sandwich shop should be nicer-smelling by now."

As they crossed the street, Jimox was pretty sure at least fifty ghosts followed.

Everything in the deli case had long before turned to worm food, then slowly dried. They knew from long experience not to touch the refrigerators and freezers, unless they planned to actually clean them out. But the back room of the little shop boasted a wide variety of canned foods neatly stacked on shelves.

"Whoopee!" Teina cheered, waving her arms. "We are RICH!"

Jimox glanced back toward the front windows, and revised his estimate upward. "A hundred now, I think. Luckily ghosts don't eat much. I think this town must have been called Spookville. I'm gonna look at the map when we get back to camp."

Teina laughed. "Spookville, original population four hundred something people, and a hundred ghosts." She started putting her favorite foods into a box. "Mmmm, sweet goma beans!"

"Spookville," Jimox took up the idea, "current population two people, and a hundred ghosts! Is that chocolate pudding?"

"Yep! And look at this — apple sauce for breakfast!"

✳

By the time Jimox and Teina had feasted and were lounging on their sleeping bags in the gift shop, evening light was beginning to fade from the sky. The map said they were in Gibson's Bay, but they had no idea who Gibson might have been. They were, however, starting to think that *more* than a hundred ghosts were haunting the former fishing village.

"Hey!" Jimox said. "We can sit by the window and read books by ghost-light!"

Teina laughed deeply. "We tried that once to save candles, remember? It didn't work."

He grinned, then crawled to the front door and pressed his face against the glass. "What d'ya think? Three hundred?"

"WHY are there three hundred ghosts in Gibson's Bay, previous population only four hundred something?" she asked. "Only a few left home with us."

"I don't know! We've been picking up more every day. They must like us."

Teina joined Jimox at the glass door. Outside in the near-darkness, more red-tinged misty shapes constantly joined those already swirling in the street. Sometimes they spilled out onto the pier, but the center of activity was clearly the little gift shop. "You're right. It's us. But WHY?"

Jimox shook his head. "I sense confusion, anger, and lots of frustration. But it's all vague, like they're here because of us, but it's not directed AT us . . . you know . . . personally."

Teina sighed. "At least they're not coming in here. I just see the same four."

His eyes opened wide. "This shop would get *really* full if all those ghosts came in *here!*"

Teina tried to relax on her sleeping bag, but was constantly aware of the ghostly shapes outside, and was beginning to think she could hear them as well, a low roaring sound mixed with moans and groans. She tried putting her fingers in her ears.

"I can hear them too," Jimox said, licking his spoon clean and putting away his can opener.

She gave up on fingers in her ears. "We're not gonna get any sleep, are we?"

He looked outside again. "Nope."

An hour later, both young monkey mammals sat at the glass window, looking out at the night sky swarming with six or seven hundred angry spirits. They had already discussed everything they knew about ghosts from their childhoods, what they had figured out by watching and listening over the last five years, and what little they had been able to read in books.

"Unfinished business?" Teina posed.

"In Gibson's Bay? *What* business?"

She shook her head.

"Seeking justice after being murdered?" he tossed out.

"All of them?" she asked in reply. "And what are *we* supposed to do about it?"

He shrugged.

After a long silence, filled only by the soft roar of hundreds of angry ghosts swirling through the little sea-side town, Teina took a slow, deep breath. "I think we should tell them."

"Tell them what?"

"Everything we've been saying."

He thought for a moment. "Worth a try, I guess."

*

They stood in the middle of the dark street full of ghostly forms, held hands and tails, and trembled. A huge swarm of buzzing anger and resentment swirled around them on all sides.

"Where should I start?" Teina asked.

"I don't know. But we can't back out now."

"No. Then they *would* come into the gift shop and drive us nuts. I'm thinking."

"Maybe just . . . you know . . . let them know we hear them."

Teina, who had once been an ordinary six-year-old girl, and in the years since then had found strength in herself she never imagined she had, took a deep breath, cupped her hands around her mouth to amplify her voice, and spoke to the angry souls swirling around them. "WE . . . HEAR . . . YOU!"

The reaction was immediate. The swarm of ghosts slowed, quieted, and softened their color from angry red to a slightly less threatening red-orange.

"Want me to do one?" Jimox asked.

"Sure."

He cupped his hands. "WE . . . FEEL . . . YOUR . . . ANGER!"

Again, the ghosts slowed and quieted, and became merely orange with frustration.

"I think they're getting interested," Teina said, "and I think I know what I want to say next."

He squeezed her tail with his.

"WE . . . DIDN'T . . . DO . . . IT!" she called loudly and clearly.

"WE . . . DIDN'T . . . EITHER!" boomed a thousand irritated voices all at once, sending the two young monkey mammals stumbling backward across the street until they landed in the gutter in front of the gift shop.

*

Teina and Jimox whimpered in each other's arms for several minutes as they slowly collected their wits and carefully determined that neither of them had broken any bones. Scrapes and bruises, however, were plentiful and tender.

The only good part was that the host of angry spirits was no longer swirling around their heads. All the frustrated ghosts were still present in the village, but seemed to be waiting for something, and while waiting, were slowly moving around the pier and the grocery store, as much as around the two travelers.

Jimox was in favor of getting inside and tending their wounds.

Teina wasn't ready to do that, and wore a thoughtful frown. Eventually she spoke her mind. "They said *We didn't either*. They feel guilty."

"But we're a thousand miles from the Gosa Desert and that secret germ-warfare lab!"

"It doesn't matter. For some reason, they *feel* guilty."

"Okay, I see your point. Maybe it's just because they voted for the last president, who pushed every military thing he could think of, including ... you know."

"I want to talk to them again."

Jimox raised his eyebrows.

"But this time, we'll be ready for their reaction."

"You want me to get sand bags and concrete blocks?"

She punched him lightly in the shoulder.

"Ouch! That's one of my bruises!"

"Sorry. Would you stand behind me, feet planted like we're expecting a wave on the beach?"

"You got it. I still think a few sand bags might be a good idea."

She grinned at him, and he grinned back.

✳

Teina walked bravely back to the middle of the street.

Jimox got behind her.

She cupped her hands. "I ... WANT ... TO ... ASK ... YOU ... SOMETHING!"

The thousand or more sparkling orange lights resumed swarming around the two little monkey mammals.

"Get ready," she whispered to Jimox. "DID ... YOU ... MAKE ... THE ... PLAGUE?"

"NO!" came a ghostly wind that threatened to return the travelers to the gutter.

With Jimox' help, Teina held her ground. "THEN ... YOU ... HAVE ... NOTHING ... TO FEEL ... GUILTY ... ABOUT!"

The young mortals were amazed at the change. The swirling hoard lost most of its anger and frustration, with only a slight tinge of yellow confusion remaining. They ceased swirling, and nearly stopped all motion, as if waiting and listening.

"Wow," she breathed.

To his eyes, she looked exhausted. "Want me to take your idea a step further?"

"Sure. I'm out of ideas."

"I ... AM ... JIMOX. THIS ... IS ... TEINA. TO ... US ... YOU ... ARE ... INNOCENT ... AND ... FREE!"

The host of spirits let out a huge sigh of relief that almost knocked the two monkey mammals off their feet, then rose into the sky while turning a beautiful blue color. Slowly, they vanished into the dark clouds.

After a long minute of silence, as they stood alone in the street and tried to catch their breath, Teina finally found her voice. "Shall we go dig out our first-aid ointment?"

"Yeah."

✳   ✳   ✳

Teina coughed deeply and reached for her water bottle. Jimox rubbed her back tenderly.

A large bird whizzed by in a child's wagon, pushed by a blue lizard. "My turn!" the reptile called, nearly out of breath.

Jimox glanced at the passing pair of friends, a gleam of pride in his old eyes. "Not all the ghosts left Gibson's Bay, you have to understand."

"We already knew all the *normal* reasons ghosts haunt places," Teina explained. "Some of those were still there, including the handful in the gift shop."

"But . . ." Mati pondered, "those weren't so angry?"

"Right," Jimox verified. "They were just stuck, for one reason or another. The old lady who ran the place, whose husband had died two years before the plague, didn't watch the news so she didn't really know what was going on, but she just couldn't imagine doing anything but running her little shop. She was stuck.

"After the *thousand* left, the local ghosts, about a dozen of them, started talking to us. Actually, only some of them could talk loud enough for us to hear, but they could all talk to each other, so they relayed messages. Lots of little personal stories, and some were able to move on after we listened to them, but nothing that added to our understanding of what had happened six years earlier."

Teina nodded. "We'll always remember Gibson's Bay, and we've marked part of it for preservation, because that's where we learned the second of our four life purposes."

"The first was being witnesses, and keeping journals," Sata remembered.

Teina nodded and smiled at the young response-ship crew member.

"We've had missions," Boro began, "where we didn't have the *foggiest* idea what we were doing for a long time!"

Teina coughed again. "Please tell us about one. We're all talked out."

Jimox nodded.

"Lyceum?" Boro proposed, glancing at his shipmates.

They all nodded or grinned.

"We had just gotten this advanced training supervisor, one mission before, who *loved* to let us figure out everything for ourselves . . ."

✳   ✳   ✳

Chapter 14: The Haunted Lodge

During the night, as Teina and Jimox slept in their favorite chamber in Fairy Castle, ships quietly trickled in from all over Nebador. The station hosts were kept busy assigning landing circles, and each ship was sternly reminded that the original hosts didn't want a fuss of any kind for their sake.

✳

After the two elderly monkey mammals shared a quiet breakfast that was more medicine than food, they eventually wandered out to the Goblin Fountain to see if anyone wanted to hear stories.

The crew of the Manessa Kwi, three young students from the Education Service, and a few others awaited them, sitting on the ground in the shade of a large tree.

Teina smiled. "I'm glad we decided not to tell anyone else."

Neither she nor Jimox saw the little video camera that allowed hundreds of other Nebador citizens around the planet station to watch and listen.

The pair got comfortable on a bench near the fountain.

"We told them about Gibson's Bay, right?" Teina asked with a frown, struggling to remember.

Many of the listeners nodded.

"I guess we should skip forward a little," Jimox suggested. "All the coastal towns were about the same after that, until . . ."

They looked at each other.

"The lodge that ate monkey mammals!" Teina suddenly remembered with wide eyes.

✳ ✳ ✳

"Weee!" Teina called as they coasted down the long stretch of road, steep enough to keep them going, not so steep as to need brakes.

Jimox stood up tall on his pedals. "No trees or branches on the road anywhere in sight!"

Teina glanced at him, and noticed how handsome he was with the wind in his fur.

A few minutes later, the road finally flattened out, forcing them to pedal again.

"That made the uphill-side worth it!" she declared.

"Yeah, not like those down-hills that are covered with junk and we almost need a shovel . . ."

"Or so steep we have to ride the brakes constantly . . ."

"Or full of pot holes . . ."

"Or with a pack of dogs halfway down we have to battle!"

They coasted to a stop at a road junction, still laughing, and looked at the sign beside the smaller road that went inland.

"Paradise Lodge," Jimox read.

"Almost a hundred years old," Teina added.

"Ocean view."

"Dining room."

"Forest trails."

"Wildlife viewing."

"Only ten minutes from here!"

Teina scowled. "That was by car, silly!"

He grinned. "I know. Shall we check it out?"

She returned his grin.

＊

Two hours later, after walking their bicycles up the steepest road they had ever seen, the pair came to the weedy parking lot, completely empty of cars.

"Good sign," Jimox said, catching his breath. "Maybe no one was here to light fires."

It had not been raining, but all around them trees dripped from the fog off the ocean. A rushing stream could be heard but not yet seen. The paved path promised to take visitors to Paradise Lodge, its heavy timber structure and mossy roof just visible through the trees.

＊

Someone had been home, and had started a fire, but luckily in a separate cabin farther down the path. The car beside it had also burned and was now just a rusting scrap heap. Several trees had been scorched, but not killed.

Jimox and Teina turned and looked at the grand old wooden lodge beside the path, its heavy double-doors awaiting their pull.

"Red flag," Jimox whispered.

Teina quickly scanned in all directions. "What?"

"Nothing, just that our heads are in the clouds."

Teina nodded and pulled out her gun. "Head back on shoulders. Perimeter check."

Jimox nodded and readied his pistol.

Walking all the way around the lodge, they found no signs that animals had found a way in, so they returned to the entrance and carefully pulled on the heavy wooden doors.

The lobby's large windows faced the ocean, giving plenty of light, and the fog appeared to be clearing. Finding no animal signs or smells, they brought in the bicycles, but searched the entire lodge, on all four levels, to be sure nothing lurked within.

The recreation room on the lowest level, and the dining room above the lobby, also had large windows toward the ocean. The Royal Suite and the Bridal Suite on the top floor shared the western side of the building. All other guest rooms looked east into the misty forest.

They chose the Royal Suite.

The kitchen was well-stocked with canned and packaged foods, and only one low shelf had been violated by rodents. The refrigerators and freezers, luckily, hadn't leaked their putrid contents. Teina found a roll of tape and strapped them tightly, just to be sure.

The resident ghosts quickly came out, all seven of them, most from the early days of the lodge almost a century before. Four or five had voices Jimox and Teina could hear, and none of them were angry or frustrated. One moved on after sharing his story with the pair of monkey mammals, and another after they listened to her story three times, relayed through another ghost.

The only angry ghost was in the burned cabin. He had been the caretaker, and had ordered the lodge closed and the staff dismissed as soon as the plague began. He had hoped he'd be safe there, miles from the nearest other person.

Jimox revealed that they were the only two people alive, and Teina assured him that he was without blame or guilt. He rose into the sky humming a little tune, and was never again seen or heard in the little burned cabin.

Jimox and Teina could never remember being so happy. They walked in the woods, dipped water out of the crystal-clear stream, and cooked their meals from a propane tank so big it would supply all their needs for years, maybe decades. No dogs roamed the woods, the wild creatures were rarely seen and had no taste for monkey mammals with guns, and all the remaining ghosts were there by choice.

The pair completely forgot about their journey to the big city in the south.

✳   ✳   ✳

"That was the lodge that ate monkey mammals," Teina declared.

Everyone laughed.

"Sounds like a serious trap," Kibi said, grinning. "How did you get away?"

"The place had cast a spell on us!" Jimox continued after grinning back at Kibi but not yet answering her question. "Time seemed to have stopped. The weather was always about the same — a little warm rain, some fog, beautiful afternoons and evenings looking out over the ocean. Suddenly, three months after we arrived, we looked around the kitchen and realized we had only enough food for about two more days!"

Kolarrr'ka stretched his wings. "Reality came knocking."

"We were in shock," Teina admitted. "We had never made a mistake like that before."

"We hadn't even checked before then," Jimox continued, "but the nearest grocery store was almost *thirty* kilometers away!"

Several listeners moaned.

"For about a minute," Jimox went on, "we considered hunting for our food. Then we remembered how few animals roamed the area, and how little we knew about hunting."

Teina smiled. "Yeah, just about nothing. The ghosts wondered why we were in such a hurry, but we had to pack and say good-bye before we starved to death!"

T'sss'lisss' eyes sparkled from Sata's shoulder, and her tail, coiled in Boro's lap, quivered with humor.

"One ghost decided to come with us, lived here for a long time, then moved on," Jimox shared. "We'll never forget Giona. We think she had something to do with the spell we were under, as she turned out to be much smarter and more powerful than all the other ghosts."

Teina took a slow breath, then added, "Paradise Lodge is now one of the planet station's retreats."

"The Nebador Preservation Specialists sprayed some clear stuff on the roof and walls that makes things last almost forever."

"We call them *The Roofers*," Teina explained with a grin. "They have their own ship, and just hover while they spray."

"All the other retreats have had *The Roofers* come, and everything in Similand too, or it wouldn't have lasted. But back to our story."

The audience got comfortable again.

"Reality forced us back onto the road," Jimox admitted. "We were sad for a couple of days, but got over it."

"It was good for us!" Teina added. "We vowed to never make *that* mistake again, and started discussing what conditions and supplies a place would have to have to be our new home, and keep us from . . . you know . . . heading back north the following year."

Jimox nodded. "So when we finally, about a month later, glimpsed the tall buildings of downtown Westron for the first time, we were ready to ask questions . . ."

✻　✻　✻

Chapter 15: Westron

A suburb on the ocean, within sight of the great city, offered plenty of good scrounging, and the trio of travelers quickly found street and motorway maps. The board room at the top of a twelve-story office building allowed them to survey the situation.

Out on the rooftop patio, once reserved for monkey mammals in suits, they leaned on the railing and watched the setting sun turn the windows of the distant skyscrapers several shades of pink and orange.

Giona's voice was very small, so Jimox and Teina couldn't be sure they got her name right, but she seemed happy with it. The pair of mortals had read about intelligent ghosts, but had never before experienced one that wasn't either stuck somewhere, or craving to move on to . . . whatever awaited them in a better place. Giona seemed to fit into neither category. She danced on the patio railing as the sun found the western horizon.

Jimox and Teina went inside to make some dinner.

A few minutes later, Giona noticed they were gone and dashed in to see what they were having.

*

The morning sun in the east brought a new, more practical perspective to the next phase of the journey. The skyscrapers were now just silhouettes, so the two monkey mammals lowered their eyes and considered the miles between here and there.

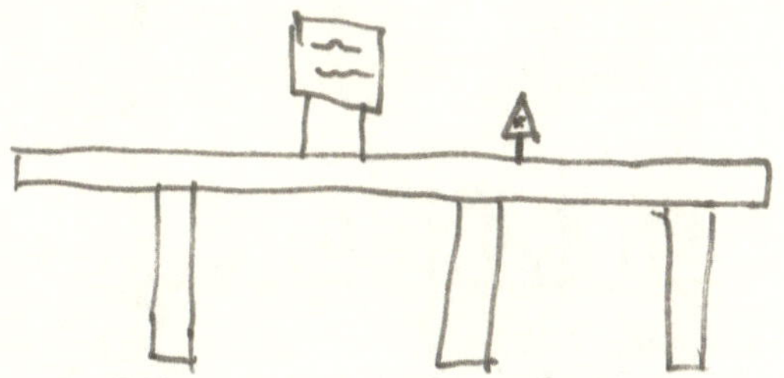

An elevated motorway began not far from their office building. Teina followed it with her spyglass. "Looks like it goes right to downtown. I've never been in a city this big."

"When I was here with my parents, we went everywhere in trains, sometimes underground."

"Best I can tell," Teina said, holding in a grin while still looking through her spyglass, "they're not running."

Jimox waited a second, then burst out snickering.

Giona, barely visible in the daylight, seemed to love the joke, and danced for joy on the patio railing.

Although they sometimes had to walk, even carry their bicycles when they came to wrecked or burned cars, they soon discovered the motorway had several advantages.

The streets below seldom went straight from anywhere to anywhere, and the map confirmed that such a journey would be long and winding. Thick weeds and overgrown bushes added to the tangle. Some of the surface streets were so choked with burned cars that passage, except on foot, appeared impossible.

Also, packs of wild dogs roamed everywhere. Giona squeaked something that might have been *monsters*. But to everyone's delight, the dogs never seemed to get up to the elevated motorway.

"There's nothing to eat up here," Jimox speculated, "except two monkey mammals they don't know about. And no water . . . or shade."

Teina nodded as she scowled at the ruined, burned city below. "I can't decide which is uglier — up here, or down there. Did we really come all this way just for *this?*"

Jimox cringed. "Um . . . we came all this way to see what we could see. If we decide to go back home, we'll do it *knowing* what's here, instead of always just wondering."

Teina nodded, stepped back from the railing, and looked east, toward the skyscrapers that were getting taller as the travelers got closer.

Like a strand of a spider's web, the motorway approached downtown, then joined another that completely encircled the heart of the great city. Empty streets and walkways, like canyons in desert badlands, carved their way into the very middle, dark and shadowy.

"They're waiting," Giona whispered, but neither monkey mammal heard her tiny voice.

The arrangement of motorways quickly gave Jimox and Teina an idea. They didn't feel ready to explore the heart of the city, and agreed that when they did so, it would be on foot. So they decided to just follow the elevated motorways around the city until they spotted something that looked safe and homey.

A sprawling steel and glass convention center looked as cozy as a parking lot. The nearby hotels were as inviting as bee hives.

Next, hundreds of warehouses marched in line, street after street, silent and still. Most were tightly closed and locked to protect things no one would ever buy again. A few had burned.

A tangled motorway interchange forced the travelers to stare at the map, trying to figure out which elevated road went where. Like a ball of knotted string, it was only unraveled after they followed each strand with a pencil.

They warily entered a short tunnel that took them in the right direction, pistols and flashlights in easy reach. From a burned car in the darkest part came the growl of a mother dog and the whimpering of puppies. The dog stayed hidden, so the travelers slipped by without stopping.

Giona came floating along behind, humming a little tune that no mortal ears could hear.

After pedaling for a few more minutes, a cultural area came into view, with a library, city hall, court house, and music hall. Gardens and small parks in between the buildings were weedy and overgrown, but still somewhat green.

"This is starting to look a little more interesting," Teina declared, dismounting after scanning the area.

Jimox joined her at the motorway railing, but faced the other direction to keep watch, pistol in hand. "Maybe we can learn more about the plague in city hall."

"I hope so," she said, focusing her spyglass. "Way fewer dogs than in the suburbs."

Jimox started swatting at something buzzing around his head.

"Mosquito?" Teina inquired, lowering the spyglass.

"Oops, sorry Giona," Jimox said, "I didn't know it was you. It's hard to see you in the daylight. Teina, I think she wants to show us something."

The barely-seen spirit, still spinning and making the loudest sound she could, led them to the far side of the motorway, forcing them to climb over the center divider.

Teina noticed Jimox keeping watch to the east, so she kept an eye on the west. "I wonder what's so important . . ."

They came to the far railing, on the side away from downtown, and beheld the city's grand old railway station. Set among towering shade trees, it appeared completely intact.

* * *

Chapter 16: Judgment Day

"Somehow, Giona knew we were going to need a safe place to return to," Jimox explained to all those seated at his feet, listening. "That beautiful old train station gave us everything we needed for nearly two weeks. Hardly more than a few ants had gotten in to bother the food and drink stacked up in two restaurants and several snack bars."

Teina brightened at the memory. "It's still used today by anyone from Nebador studying old downtown Westron."

"So we set up camp in the station," Jimox continued, "then worked up enough courage to poke our noses into the city. At first, the streets and walkways between the skyscrapers were dark and mysterious to us . . ."

Teina grinned.

"But we soon learned that we were as safe as we could be . . . and eventually we learned why."

⁕ ⁕ ⁕

Jimox stood in the middle of a silent street between massive buildings, peering into the shadows ahead with his spyglass.

Teina scanned in all directions, and frowned at several artistic murals within sight, all about machines, wires, motorways, or other things hard and ugly.

"Dog two blocks down," Jimox reported. "Nope, it just whined and took off, away from us."

"Weird," Teina commented. "Have you seen Giona?"

"Not since we left the station."

"Two more blocks, then circle back to the mayor's office?"

"Sounds good," he replied and lowered his spyglass.

⁕

The contest between the city hall's security system, and Jimox' pry bars, wasn't a fair fight. Batteries that hadn't been charged in seven years complained weakly, then fell silent. Metal detectors, by themselves, could do nothing. Polished brass locks looked nice, but broke easily.

Teina started with the mayor's desk itself. After shuffling through papers for a while, she stopped and read one carefully. "What's a . . .

R-E-F-U-G-E-E," she asked.

Jimox, working through a filing cabinet, defined the word.

"Well, they had a camp for them, out in the desert, and told everyone the plague wouldn't get there, but it did."

"The *Gosa* Desert? That's where they *invented* it!"

Teina laughed. "No, different desert. But that's it. Everything else here . . . we already know about from other offices."

Jimox closed the filing cabinet drawer with a bang. "Nothing in here either. I bet he didn't have a . . . what did they call it? . . . a *need-to-know*. He was just the mayor of one of the biggest cities in the world — no one important."

Teina could feel her friend's frustration, so she sat down on the floor beside him. "We know things none of them *ever* knew."

"Like what?" Jimox asked with almost a pout.

"Like which kinds of cookies are still good after all these years, and how to talk to ghosts and give them a chance to move on, and how to be happy even though we're the only two people in the world!"

Jimox tried to smile.

Teina grabbed his tail with hers and squeezed until he took a deep breath and was ready to head back into the city.

✳

Another week passed as they explored more sections of downtown Westron, and riffled through every office that might have known anything about the plague.

Each evening, they returned to the train station to relax, make a tasty meal, and look over official memos, tourist pamphlets, and anything else interesting they had found that day.

Giona was often there, and quickly introduced the sixteen ghosts who called the station home. One was freed from his worldly bonds just by Teina saying hello and repeating back his name. Three more moved on after the pair of monkey mammals listened to their stories of life, and then death.

While out and about in the city, the pair was sometimes warned by loud squawks and threatening swoops when they got too near some bird's nest, but never, during their entire stay in downtown Westron, did they have to fend off a single dog. As yet, they had no idea why.

✳

A day came when they had no plan, but didn't feel like staying at the train station, so they wandered aimlessly through the empty streets. The city was even more silent than usual, seeming to soak up the very sounds of their footsteps. A funny color crept into the sky, but so little of it was visible from street level that the pair of monkey mammals didn't notice.

Slowly, Teina became aware that the fur on the back of her neck was tingling. She looked behind them several times, but saw nothing.

Giona appeared suddenly, and clearly wanted them to follow. They looked at each other.

Jimox raised his eyebrows. "She's never steered us wrong before."

Teina shrugged. She was curious, but another feeling, under the surface, was trying to make itself known.

Two blocks later, they came to a tiny park, just a little triangle of weeds where three streets came together at an odd angle. Barely visible among the weeds sat a lone bench, upon which Giona danced.

Jimox smiled. "A one-bench park."

"Looks like this is where she wanted us to go. Why do I feel . . ."

"What?"

"What's that phrase they use in comic books? Oh, yeah — *impending doom*."

Jimox quickly scanned in all directions. "Nothing visible . . . except . . . uh oh . . ."

"WHAT!"

Jimox still didn't find his voice, so Teina stepped to his side and looked in the direction he was facing.

About half a block away, from the street level to about ten stories up, the air was full of ghosts. Most visible in the deepest shadows of the buildings, they had that red tint that Jimox and Teina had seen before.

They both swallowed, linked tails, and slowly turned. Down every other street that converged on the tiny park, they beheld the same sight. As they turned all the way back to the first street, they realized the angry, frustrated spirits were getting closer.

"Guess what *we're* doing today," Jimox whispered.

"Good thing we didn't have any other plans. You didn't leave cookies baking or anything, did you? This could take a while."

Jimox chuckled. "I think . . . Giona's been busy, you know, arranging things."

"This is lots more than we had at Gibson's Bay. What, a million?"

"At least. You're better at this than I am. I'll be your sand bags."

"Huh! Forget it, bucko. You're at my side, helping me talk to them, or we're running."

"You can't run from ghosts!"

Teina grinned at him.

"Okay, okay, I'm thinking."

"Let's . . . relax . . ." she began thoughtfully, "sit on the bench . . . let them come to us."

"I like that. It might help my heart to quit racing."

✳   ✳   ✳

"At Gibson's Bay," Teina began after a deep cough, "we talked to maybe a thousand ghosts who had gathered from several small cities farther inland. This was different. Twelve or thirteen million monkey mammals had lived . . . and died . . . in Westron, or the refugee camps in the desert nearby." Almost out of breath, she stopped and looked at Jimox.

"And some of them were still there, wanting us to pass judgment . . ."

"The only problem was . . ." Teina said excitedly, but then lost her breath.

"The only problem was," Jimox took up the thought, "they weren't all innocent."

A murmur of surprise rippled through the listeners.

"There were actually two groups of ghosts around us at that tiny little triangular park. The masses of people were angry and frustrated, but also a small group of sickly dull-green ghosts seemed to be . . . prisoners."

"We have no idea how ghosts can keep other ghosts captive," Teina added, "but they did."

"So we had to figure out how to be lawyers and judges *fast!*"

*   *   *

One of the green captives was forced to come forward and grovel before Jimox and Teina.

"Um . . ." Jimox began, sensing it was his turn, "what part did you play in making the plague germs?"

The million or more shimmering spirits fell completely silent and listened.

Eventually a tiny voice was heard. "Laboratory assistant."

The assembled masses roared for revenge.

Teina raised her hand, and silence returned. "Did you have any say in what was made in that laboratory?"

"No."

The ghostly audience hissed, but fell silent when Jimox looked at them. "Do any of you have evidence that this one is lying?"

No one responded.

Teina reached out to touch the dull-green ghost, but felt only cold air. "You, little one, are innocent."

The host of angry spirits roared and swirled around the tiny park, but

Teina stood up and crossed her arms. "You asked us to judge, and release you from guilt if you were innocent! Now either listen to us, or find someone else!"

Jimox, at her side, hooked his tail with hers, and could feel her trembling.

From somewhere nearby, they thought they heard Giona giggle.

The million grumbled for another minute, but slowly relaxed and pushed another green captive forward.

As they sat back down, Jimox whispered, "There *is* no one else. They're stuck with us."

Teina nodded and looked at the new captive. "What part did you play at the secret laboratory in the Gosa Desert?"

The groveling spirit twisted this way and that, but said nothing.

"If you don't answer *us*, then we'll have to leave you with *them*," Jimox warned.

The ghost turned almost black before whispering, "Director of Research."

Teina frowned, but decided to ask the question anyway. "Could you have stopped what happened?"

The spirit became even darker, and said nothing.

Millions of watchers buzzed with anger.

Jimox took a deep breath. "I don't think there's any way we can find this one innocent."

"But . . . how do you punish a ghost?" Teina wondered, just loud enough for Jimox to hear. "We can't put it in jail, or sentence it to *death*."

Jimox snickered for a moment, then his eyes lit up with an idea. "How about . . . community service?"

Teina's face twisted in thought. "Ghost-style community service, whatever that might be."

The red and orange million swirled and roared for revenge.

"Shut up so we can think!" Teina yelled.

Silence instantly fell throughout the entire city. Jimox was absolutely sure that not even an insect dared buzz.

"Your call," she prodded.

Jimox closed his eyes for a moment, then realized he had to do two things — punish the guilty, and satisfy the crowd. "Um . . . these thousands and thousands of innocent spirits will be moving on to ... a better place ... just as soon as all this business is finished. You will not ...."

The guilty ghost twisted with torment.

The listeners sighed and turned a soft yellow color.

"I think you're on the right track," Teina whispered.

Jimox' mind raced. "You will stay here and help other ghosts, who are stuck for any reason, to move on. If you do this well for ...." He looked at Teina. "What do you think, a thousand years?"

"That seems harsh."

"Hundred?"

She nodded.

"If you do it well for a hundred years, then you will be released."

The crowd started buzzing.

Jimox raised his voice. "If you do it poorly, or fail to learn your lesson, then it will automatically become a thousand years."

The million assembled spirits relaxed and seemed satisfied.

✳

Thirty-seven more dull-green prisoners were pushed forward, and the pair of monkey mammals dispensed justice quickly, now that they knew what they were doing. Most were innocent, just doing their jobs and having no say in the project goals and no idea what the consequences would be. Five more were sentenced to a hundred years of ghostly community service, a thousand if they screwed up.

Finally, the time came for Jimox and Teina to give all the innocent spirits their blessing to move on to whatever awaited them. The collective sigh of relief nearly shook the buildings of downtown Westron as most of them floated upward into the sky.

✳

The pair of monkey mammals looked around. The process had taken so long that evening had descended upon the city, the sky was rapidly darkening, and the million ghosts were no longer present to cast their eerie half-light.

A few spirits remained, perhaps a hundred, none of them red with anger or yellow with frustration. They filtered away into nearby buildings where they seemed to have attachments.

Giona was still present, dancing on the back of the bench, shimmering a proud golden color.

Jimox and Teina suddenly felt completely exhausted and ravenously hungry. They fished in their day packs and drained little bottles of juice.

Jimox tried his flashlight. "Batteries are dead. They were good this morning!"

"Mine too," Teina moaned. Then she looked at Giona. "You got us into this. I hope you'll guide us home."

"Weeee!" Giona squeaked and danced away up the street.

*

Three times on the way back to the train station, dogs threatened the pair as they followed their ghostly guide through the darkness, hands and tails linked for courage. All three times, several dull-green ghosts descended upon the wild canines and sent them away, yelping for their lives.

* * *

Chapter 17: Similand

On a beautiful spring morning, two days after judging and releasing a million or more ghosts, Teina and Jimox blinked and stretched as they lay in their sleeping bags and gazed up at the ornate ceiling, a good ten meters above them, of the grand old train station. With morning light angling through doors on the east side of the building, Teina rolled onto her belly and grabbed the city map. Jimox wiggled close to look at it with her.

"Let's see . . ." she began, "in the last two weeks, we've explored downtown Westron 'til we're sick of it . . ."

Jimox chuckled and nodded.

". . . unless you can think of any other places there might be . . . you know . . . information."

"Hmm . . ." he pondered with a wrinkled brow. "We've read all the memos on the mayor's desk, the police chief's office, the fire chief, and spent an entire *day* in Emergency Services . . ."

"And hardly learned *anything* we didn't already know."

He rolled onto his back. "I'm still trying to put all the pieces together. If Emergency Services knew the plague had gotten into the refugee camps in the desert, why didn't they tell the local leaders, so they could announce it and people would quit going there?"

"Mmmmm . . . probably because that would look bad? Who was it who told people to go there in the first place?"

Jimox laughed. "Okay, I get it. Saving face was more important than saving people."

Teina shrugged, then grabbed the thick stack of tourist pamphlets and gave half to Jimox. "Some of these are a long ways away."

"Okay, this pile is for those. And we need a pile for things that might be dangerous, like the zoo."

"I hope someone opened the cages before Burning Day," she said with sympathy. "Well, part of me hopes so."

Jimox nodded. "And a bunch of places are just little things, like famous houses."

Teina added several to that pile. "I'd like to see some of those, you know, when we're in the neighborhood."

"Things on islands go in the *far-away* pile," Jimox said.

"Those might as well be on another *planet*. And we've seen everything in downtown Westron," Teina said, starting a new pile.

A few minutes later, they had them all sorted, and only one pamphlet didn't fit anywhere. Teina looked at it with sparkling eyes.

Jimox, who had a faint memory of it from childhood, looked at his younger friend, who had never had the experience. "Shall we ... say good-bye to our beautiful train station and wander down toward Similand?"

Teina grinned and wiggled with excitement.

✳

After instant cereal and dried fruit, they packed all their extra food into buckets, stacked them on tables mice couldn't climb, and made sure all the windows and doors would keep out birds and dogs.

The handful of resident ghosts, who had reasons of their own for lingering in the old station, watched the pair of visitors prepare to depart, and sometimes let themselves be seen.

When the pair was ready, Jimox faced the ghosts who were hovering near the ticket counter. "Thank you for letting us stay in your beautiful train station. Like we said before, you are free and innocent, but it is not for us to say whether you stay or go."

Teina nodded and waved to them.

The ghostly forms dashed into their favorite hiding places.

Giona danced on the handle bars of Teina's bicycle.

✳

Although summer was not far off, a cool breeze from the ocean met the pair as they pushed their bicycles through the heavy doors, letting them close and latch.

Teina looked back at the century-old building. "Nice to know we have a good stash in a safe place."

Jimox checked the pistol in his handle-bar basket, mounted, and began pedaling toward the street. "Wasn't there a motorway entrance just down the street?"

Teina mounted. "Yeah. We have to go east a little, then south."

✳

The breeze died down and the day became warm, compared to what they were used to in the far north, even though the clouds remained thick and threatened rain.

The motorway had three or four lanes on each side, so even when the travelers came to tangles of rusting cars, they seldom had to stop.

Bleached bones, monkey mammal or dog, sometimes made them walk their bicycles a short distance, with guns handy and eyes and ears wide open for danger.

About noon, a pack of scrawny brown dogs blocked the road, but they were weak and skittish, and one warning shot sent them away, whining.

The miles passed slowly. The motorway, and the burned or crumbing buildings beyond, were most often ugly and uninviting. Somewhere just past Exit 117, a large black dog refused to give way. After a well-aimed shot, Jimox and Teina hurried on before other dogs came for the fresh meat.

As the pair waited under a bridge during a rain shower, Teina looked at the map. "About two more miles."

Jimox finished reloading. "This city seems to go on forever. Can you imagine what it was like with everyone setting fires?"

Teina thought for a moment. "No. Very glad I wasn't here."

Jimox nodded.

✳

They first beheld the World Tree after pedaling under another bridge, the Tree's great limbs of steel and concrete, and leaves of plastic, reaching for the sky. Stairs, ramps, climbing ropes, slides, water flumes, and roller coaster tracks laced themselves from branch to branch, giving the impression that a giant spider had spun webs all over the massive tree. Little else of the world's largest amusement park could be seen from outside.

Teina coasted to a stop and stared in amazement.

Jimox knew it was her first glimpse of Similand, so he took watch and scanned for dangers.

"It's . . . wonderful," she began, "but very eerie because it's so quiet and still. You just *can't* have a tree like that without every kid for a hundred miles *begging* to play on it, day and night."

Jimox, whose expertise consisted of one visit at age eight, nodded. "It was open 'til midnight, and people would linger in the souvenir shops and restaurants 'til one or two."

"How do we . . . get in?"

"This is the back side. We have to take the next motorway exit, then we'll come to the front. I guess . . . tickets are free today."

Teina grinned at him.

✳

The huge parking lot contained only weeds busy enlarging the cracks.

The entry plaza was ringed by silent ticket booths, dark snack bars, locked gift shops, empty pet kennels, and unattended information desks.

In the west, the sun prepared to set, casting orange light over everything and giving the place a little bit of the magical glow it had once possessed.

The pair cautiously walked their bicycles, scanning for two things at once — all the usual dangers, and anything that might still be fun even without the music, lights, motorized movement, and costumed employees that once filled the theme park.

Jimox had been right. No one stopped him from hopping over a turnstile and unlatching the exit gate so they could roll their bicycles in.

Shadows rapidly became longer all around them.

"We need to find somewhere safe very soon," Teina said. "Those turnstiles won't keep *anything* out."

The last time Jimox had been here, his mind had been on other matters. Now he looked around with a new purpose. The first visible ride was the Olde Towne station of the Kid's Motorway, a sturdy brick building on the small hill that encircled the park. "Up there! We'll have a good view, the station looks intact, and there's a second floor even if the ground level isn't secure."

Teina quickly spotted a ramp marked with a stroller symbol, and pushed her bicycle in that direction, all the while peering with sharp eyes into the lengthening shadows.

Jimox came behind, handle bars in one hand, pistol in the other.

*

The station was locked, but Jimox was able to spring the latch without breaking it. They rolled their bicycles in, looked at each other, and slapped hands.

With enough evening light in the sky to allow the pair to see any approaching danger on the little hill, they stepped back outside.

On the Olde Towne side of the station, ramps and stairs once held excited children standing in line. Jimox spotted one small ghost lingering near a drinking fountain, jumping up and down as if trying to get a drink, seemingly unaware that water no longer flowed there.

Below, the idyllic small town of about a hundred years before once offered every possible vintage service and period entertainment. Now, weeds filled every planter, and more were slowly working on the pavement. No lights twinkled in shop windows, and no music came from the bandstands. Teina noticed a couple of ghosts moving along a wooden sidewalk together, as if strolling hand in hand toward their favorite ice cream parlor. "Wow, this place is fantastic! Nothing's burned!"

Looking above the Olde Towne rooftops, the pair of travelers could see the World Tree in the center of the park, a couple of roller coasters off to one side, and glimpses of medieval castles beyond.

At that moment, the sun sank below the western horizon, the magical orange glow disappeared from walls, signs, decorations, and trees, and all the shadows deepened.

Jimox spotted a dog lurking under the tables of a sidewalk restaurant below. He pointed, Teina nodded, and they quickly slipped into the safety of the Kid's Motorway station.

✳   ✳   ✳

Chapter 18: Olde Towne

The ground level of the Kid's Motorway station was just a waiting room for parents, with hard benches and a vending machine. Up the narrow stair that said *Employees Only*, Teina found a comfortable little office and lounge. Jimox brought up their sleeping bags. Side by side, they knelt on a couch and pressed their faces to the window.

The fantastic World Tree, with its slides and ropes and everything else a child could want, stood in silhouette against the evening sky. From this height, the pair could see all the winding streets of Olde Towne, now deep in shadow.

"Sometimes I've been sad," Teina began, "when I realized the plague stole half my childhood. Now I'm in the one place in the world that *every* kid dreamed of going, and it's free, we can stay as long as we want, and none of it's burned!"

"Makes sense," Jimox said. "No one lived here. I bet they locked the place up tight when the news said the plague was out of control."

"That was three days before Burning Day."

Jimox nodded, and continued gazing at their new home as the light faded from the sky.

✳

They took the next morning to clean out the little refrigerator in the employee lounge, and salvage what they could from the vending machine downstairs.

With pistols and extra ammunition on their belts, sun hats on their heads, day packs, and a map of the theme park in hand, they began to explore.

Although only four streets wound through Olde Towne, from the ground it seemed like an endless maze, and the many balconies, foot bridges, and dead-end alleys added to the feeling of being lost in a tangled city of times past. Every possible shop, restaurant, and theater lined the streets, but all were dark and locked.

Teina kept track of their location on the map, and Jimox watched for dogs. Only one showed its face, and dashed away after taking a good look at the tall, confident monkey mammals.

A little lunch counter once boasted varnished wood and polished brass, but now the wood was dusty and the brass tarnished. The refrigerator and freezer doors bulged open with fungus and slimy mold, and the pastry case contained something green that the pair of theme-park visitors, faces pressed to the window, couldn't name.

A theater once showed old cartoons constantly. The snack counter appeared ready to pop popcorn by the bucket, but now stood silent, waiting for Similand to open again in the morning, a morning that never came.

The furry dolls in a gift shop, based on every possible fairy-tale character, looked back at Jimox and Teina with unblinking plastic eyes.

"When I was six," Teina remembered, cupping her hands around her face to better see through the dusty glass, "I would have loved to have every doll in this store. Now . . . they just make me sad."

Jimox said nothing, but touched her shoulder gently with his tail.

Eventually they emerged from the maze of streets and stood before the great World Tree. It towered, according to the map, more than two hundred feet above them. On this side, the entrance to the ladders, ropes, and slides beckoned to the only two visitors in the park.

The child in each of them was ready to dash right in and play. Another part — the part that had kept them alive for the last seven years — was willing to wait, look, and listen.

"I think . . . today we should just do a walk-through on the ground," Jimox proposed.

"Agreed. We need to know what's lurking in this place."

Almost before Teina finished speaking, something in the huge tree jumped several feet, a bird's cry of pain was quickly cut off, and feathers came floating down.

"Cat!" she declared, shielding her eyes and looking up.

"Yeah. Dogs couldn't get up the ladders."

Nothing more of the contest could be seen, but judging from the silence, the cat had won. The pair of monkey mammals turned and looked at the entrance to the western part of Similand.

*　*　*

Chapter 19: Machineland

With few trees to drop leaves, and those nearly dead from lack of watering, the Machineland Plaza was almost clean. "We haven't seen any trash anywhere," Jimox observed.

Teina nodded. "They shut everything down, locked up, and took out the trash. Nice of them."

When they reached the center of the plaza, Jimox turned a slow circle. "Eerie. Of all places in the world, this one should be full of movement and sound. The Kid's Motorway is all around us, the Space Rockets are between those snack bars, and the Machineland Express has three stations, there, there, and there. The Bumper Cars are that way, the Flying Baskets are right behind them, the entrance to the Wild Roller Ride is up that walkway . . . and it's all completely still and silent. Very weird."

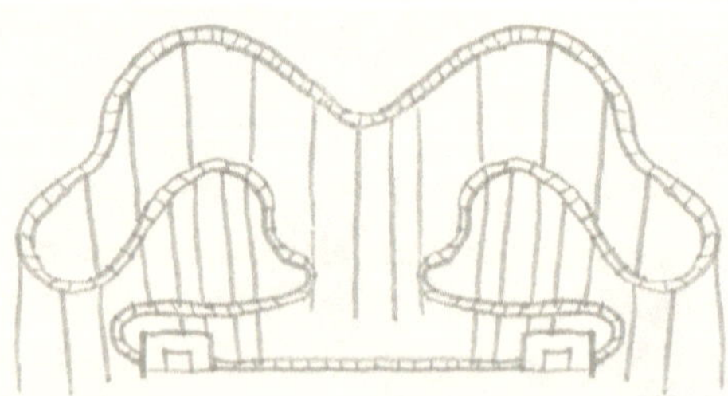

Teina studied the eating places. "Looks like mostly junk food, hot dogs and stuff. Not very good scrounging — it'll all be garbage."

They wandered among the silent rides, shuttered snack counters, and locked souvenir shops. "Could any of it be made to work again?" Teina asked.

"Not without electricity, lots and lots of electricity," Jimox replied. A moment later, he frowned in thought.

Teina noticed. "What?"

"Except . . . the roller coasters work by gravity. If you could get a car up the lift hill, like with a winch, then you could ride it down the rest of the way!"

Teina smiled, and a sparkle appeared in her eyes just knowing she might be able to experience a tiny sampling of the thrills the place once gave children from all over the world.

For a few minutes at each ride, the pair of young monkey mammals broke their own rules and indulged themselves in the mischievous dreams of every child.

They *walked* on the Kid's Motorway lanes, even the elevated sections, once forbidden to anyone but employees rushing to restart a stalled car.

The metal cables that suspended the Space Rockets, already starting to rust, creaked as they used their bodies to make the rockets swing back and forth.

They tried all the valves and levers in the engineer's cab of the Machineland Express. Nothing worked, except the bell, and it rang so loudly they cringed and dashed away, glancing around with guilty faces.

The Flying Baskets would swing and spin in place a little, but nothing else.

The Wild Roller Ride called to them also, allowing the pair to creep along catwalks, climb access ladders, and peer behind the fading plywood facades of fantasy houses and mythical creatures.

But when they gazed at the tracks that climbed the huge lift hill and tried to imagine winching a roller coaster car to the top, they looked at each other and shook their heads.

Eventually they returned to the Machineland Plaza.
"Yep," Teina agreed. "Very silent, very still, very weird."

Chapter 20: Castleland

Back at the World Tree, the pair noticed the entrances to the roller coaster and the water flume that both wound among the huge branches. Again, they took a step in that direction before stopping themselves.

Jimox sighed. "We'll have plenty of time for that."

Teina nodded, and they turned to look at the entrance to Castleland.

If Machineland was devoted to the creations of the mind, Castleland was especially for the heart. The entrance walkway mimicked tunnels under bushes that a child might creep through to discover the enchanted world within. The doors and windows of Gnome houses appeared under every rock and tree, at first very small, then larger and larger as the visitors moved forward, giving them the illusion they were shrinking. The little houses once boasted lights and sounds, Jimox explained, but were now completely silent, except that sometimes the sun angled in and illuminated tiny furniture, even pretend food on little tables.

Fairy houses dangled from tree limbs, like bird houses, and in a few, real birds had pecked through the doors and built nests.

The real trees were soon intermixed with artificial ones, which began to have faces, arms, hands, and sometimes feet. They once had voices, Jimox remembered, and parts of them moved.

Teina giggled with delight.

Three castles surrounded the Castleland Plaza — one realistic, one bright and fanciful, one dark and evil. Each could be explored on foot or in the cars of a slow-moving ride, and they all offered snack bars and gift shops.

Teina pointed to the Castle Kitchen, in its own timber building with thatched roof. "An actual restaurant! Could be good scrounging."

"I think my family ate there — closest thing to real food in all of Similand."

Just outside the Castle Kitchen, tables and benches surrounded a large stone fountain, now completely dry. The pair of explorers looked up as they slowly walked around it. "Every kind of goblin that ever was!" Teina remarked.

Several more rides filled the spaces between the castles, all small and slow for young children.

Teina quickly spotted the many walk-through or crawl-through attractions, some just a short detour into the house of a fairy-tale character, others long, winding mazes.

"This feels better," she declared. "Not everything needs electricity."

"That's what I was thinking," Jimox agreed. "And part of every castle was fixed up with real furniture, just like a fancy house."

Teina took on a mischievous grin. "I get Fairy Castle, and you get the plain one!" Then she frowned in thought. "Or maybe I want the Witch's Castle . . ."

Jimox howled with laughter.

Teina sighed and became serious. "No, I could never sleep without you nearby."

Jimox smiled shyly.

*

Flashlights in hand, they took the walk-through path for each castle.

In the realistic Knight's Castle, the lord and his lady had massive wooden furniture, thick wall hangings, and a table brimming with plastic food, while prisoners in the dungeon made do with bread and water.

The Potion Room in the Witch's Castle had more cauldrons and twisted glassware than any laboratory, and stuffed animals in cages looked on with frightened eyes. In the Witch's Chamber, the huge crystal ball once flashed with images of people and events, Jimox explained, but was now dark and silent.

Although boys might prefer the Knight's Castle, Fairy Castle was every little girl's dream. The Party Room boasted crystal dishes of every color on delicate furniture with curving legs. Jars of fairy dust and racks of wands adorned the Magic Room, where the tables and chairs all had arms and smiling faces. Finally, the Fairy King and Queen's Chamber was covered with silk and lace, with thick furs on the floor, and cut crystal windows letting in sparkling light.

Teina sighed with longing.

* * *

Chapter 21: Forestland

"Forestland is where we are now," Jimox said, gazing around with his elderly eyes. "From the pictures in the tourist pamphlets, and my memory, we knew everything used to be carefully trimmed and watered. But when *we* got here, weeds were a meter high, leaves and broken branches lay everywhere, and most plants were dead or dying."

"It took us *years* to get it looking nice!" Teina declared, then lapsed into a fit of coughing.

Jimox held her close as he pointed to different buildings. "Birds had gotten into one gift shop through a broken window, but mostly things were in good shape. Of course, we had to find the keys . . ."

Teina started laughing. "That took a month!"

Jimox smiled. "But if Machineland was a play space devoted to the creations of our minds, and Castleland was especially for our hearts, then Forestland represented the soul of our people. There were a few high-tech rides — in there, over there, and around that corner — but they were all about trees, deep woods, mountains, and caves — climbing, swinging from ropes, flying, bobsledding . . ."

"And since this is the biggest open space inside the park . . ." Teina managed to say before losing her wind.

"This is where we met Nebador," Jimox completed the thought. "But before we can tell that story, you have to hear about the thirteen-year-old girl who repaired and re-designed an entire city water system." He looked at his beloved partner and grinned.

She blushed.

✳   ✳   ✳

After spending hours in Castleland, the pair of young monkey mammals returned to the World Tree, then crunched through the dry leaves and twigs that lay years-thick all across Forestland.

Teina stared at a pair of double doors, then studied her map. "Three-D Theater, ten different shows, all from the point of view of little forest creatures that dig or fly. That would have been fun."

Jimox nodded and sighed. "Just rows of empty seats now." He turned his attention to a snack bar in a little cave.

"Served nut milks and fruity drinks," Teina announced. "Maybe some of it came in cans or bottles."

"Hope so."

Teina brightened, looking at a pair of plastic trees that bent over to form a small entrance archway. "*Here's* something that still works! Toddler's Forest Playground. Safe for all ages, it says."

Jimox frowned, forced out a smile, and followed Teina in.

After discovering they no longer fit in any of the seats in the Toddler's Forest Playground, the pair wandered on, discussing how each attraction might be useful or fun now, without employees, electricity, or fresh supplies. To make matters worse, several rides and gardens needed water, and every pond, pool, fountain, faucet, sink, and toilet was dry as a bone.

Then they heard a tiny sound.

Teina looked at her map, and indeed, just ahead should be Forestland Lake on which little boats once sailed, with splashing waterfalls, lighted fountains, and low-hanging trees to make the ride more interesting.

They heard the faint sound of trickling water.

"Red flag!" Teina whispered loudly.

Jimox had not yet realized the danger, but instantly followed one of their most sacred rules. He scanned his side of the large open area. "Stairs to an observation platform!"

Teina looked, and they moved quickly in that direction.

With guns drawn, they ascended the leaf-covered steps, and found they had the platform to themselves.

"What did you sense?" he asked as soon as they knew the place was safe.

"I realized that if there's water, then every critter in the park is going to be there, maybe whole packs of them."

Jimox' eyes grew wide, and together they walked to the far end of the platform, overlooking Forestland Lake.

It was empty, but the bottom was green with marsh grasses.

Teina pulled a spyglass from her day pack. "Far left end, a pipe with a trickle of water coming out. Birds trying to get a drink. A brown dog trying to catch a bird. Uh oh, big gray dog creeping closer. Brown dog sees him, is standing his ground."

"I can hear them growling."

While the dogs fought, and the birds used the opportunity to drink, the two monkey mammals watched. After a few minutes, Jimox pulled a small pry bar from his day pack, went to work on the vending machine, and soon handed Teina food and drink.

"Thanks. I'm keeping an eye on the stairs."

"I've been thinking," he said, ripping open a package of crackers. "If we're gonna stay here, you know, make this our home for more than a month or so, then we've got two big problems."

Teina chewed on dry cookies and listened.

"We have to make the outside fence animal-proof. The place was in the middle of a city, and the fence was designed to make kids pay at the front gate. It just wasn't meant to keep out a constant stream of wild dogs."

Teina nodded. "And once we got the fence all fixed, we could clean out what's in here. It wouldn't do any good right now, as more would just creep in."

"I don't see any problem with food," Jimox continued, "as there are stores and restaurants all over the city. We could *survive* with bottled water and that one tiny trickle, once we got rid of the dogs, but if we could find out where the water's coming from, and why it's just a trickle, I bet we could fix some leaks and get a lot *more* than a trickle."

"If you'll do the fence, I'll do the water!" Teina offered.

✳ ✳ ✳

"I had no idea what I was getting myself into," the elderly monkey mammal said slowly, her mind lost in far-away memories.

"Of course," Jimox explained, "both projects took years, and required both of us. I couldn't do *anything* on the fence without Teina protecting me from dogs and handing me stuff while I was up on a ladder."

"And I'd find big old valves I needed to open or close, but I wasn't strong enough." She paused to cough. "Jimox was, or knew how to use something as a lever."

"And if it hadn't been for that water system, we probably never would have met the people of Nebador."

She smiled at him.

"You see," he continued, "our water was coming from a little reservoir in the hills east of here. The dam was in good shape, so all we had to do was stop the water from leaking out at every burned house or open faucet . . . you know, all five or six million of them . . ."

* * *

Chapter 22: Thrills

The following day, the elderly pair did not appear at the Goblin Fountain. Their ursine healer came out just long enough to announce that her charges needed a day of rest.

Ashley mumbled something about the museum and wandered away.

Kolarrr'ka waddled off to interview the current station hosts.

T'sss'lisss slithered toward the Witch's Castle, curious about the little windows high-up on its dark towers.

Boro and Sata looked at each other. "Want to . . ." he began, "explore some old rides?"

"Yeah!" she replied with a very child-like grin.

Every building, ride, or play space, they already knew, began with a sign, in the language of Nebador, explaining what was within, what skills or equipment were necessary, and what dangers might befall the unprepared.

They came to the first attraction, a large opening in a thick hedge. *"Fairy Picnic Area,"* Boro read. *"Any species, any age, any handicap, no equipment needed, no dangers. Small nutrition cabinet within."*

Sata scrunched her face. "Maybe for lunch after something more exciting."

Boro nodded and they wandered into Forestland.

Sata read the next sign at a dark cave-like opening. *"Beneath-the-Forest Challenge Course. Strong arms and tail required, gloves recommended. No safety nets, extreme danger for most species."*

Boro's face turned sour. "Um . . . I wasn't thinking of anything *that* exciting."

Sata looked at him with wide eyes. "Me neither!"

Next, they came to Ice Mountain Bobsleds.

"Anyone can ride who fits in a bobsled and enjoys high speeds and

sudden inertia changes," Boro read. *"Clearance is one meter. Equines and other large species, beware."*

Sata grinned. "We work on a response ship, ride fanators, slide down water ramps . . ."

Boro nodded and continued reading. *"Step One. Make sure the pond on your left is full of water, or the bobsled won't stop and you will die."*

Their eyes snapped open wide and they hurried down the path, but relaxed when they found the pond completely full, and could see the last section of bobsled track slightly underwater.

They looked at each other and nodded.

"Step Two. Hook the lead bobsled to the winching cable."

"Got it!" Sata declared.

"Step Three. Winch the bobsled to the top of the lift hill."

For the next quarter hour, they took turns working the large crank handle as the bobsled car slowly ascended the steep section of track.

"Can you imagine what Jimox and Teina when through," Sata said while resting, "when they had to figure this out for the first time, all by themselves?"

Boro stopped cranking and let Sata take over. "That would be scary . . . and fun."

"Step Four," Boro read when Sata announced the winch would go no further. *"Climb the stairs on your right."*

While their arms rested, their legs got a good workout.

A cool breeze whistled through the simulated icy mountain pass where the bobsled car waited, less than a meter from the highest point on its track. A small shelter, made to look like an alpine cabin, once housed a Similand Safely Attendant, but now contained only a Nebador emergency medical kit.

"Step Five," Boro continued reading on a new sign, *"Attach the safety line to the bobsled."*

"Check," Sata said.

"Disconnect the winch line."

"Done."

"Push the bobsled over the hump."

Sata pushed. "Ummmmph! It's about a meter on the other side now."

"Step Eight. Climb into the bobsled."

The track the bobsled was poised to descend was much less steep than the lift hill, but quickly disappeared between boulders and into caves. Loops of track could be seen in many places on the mountainside below, but exactly how they connected, and where they went when unseen, was a complete mystery to the pair of visitors. They climbed into the bobsled cautiously, Boro stepping in first to sit in back, Sata in front, her smaller size allowing him to see.

The instructions continued at the front of the passenger compartment of the bobsled, so Sata read. *"Step Eleven. Secure your inertia straps."*

Similar to those on the Manessa Kwi, this was quickly done.

"Step Twelve. Reach back, pull slightly on the safety line, and release it. The Ice Mountain Bobsled ride will begin as soon as you let go of the safety line."

Boro carried out the last step.

The bobsled car began to move very slowly at first, but both riders knew that gravity was now in complete control, and their only hope was to somehow survive, physically and mentally, until the pond at the bottom of the simulated mountain brought them to a complete stop.

*

A glimpse of Forestland, then sudden darkness, followed seconds later by Castleland spread out far below. Faster and faster the bobsled raced down its track . . . crystals of many colors glowing in a dark cave . . . blue sky with a few puffy clouds . . . darkness with nothing but a pair of beady red eyes . . . a bright glimpse of the World Tree . . . a jerk to the right and more darkness . . .

It occurred to Sata that the bobsled instructions, unlike the fanators, hadn't said anything about screaming.

Boro's mind raced, aware that he wanted to be in control, like when he was the engineer or pilot of a response ship, but couldn't be, other than to hold on and not let any part of his body get more than a meter outside the bobsled.

A sudden jerk to the left took them into darkness again, with many pairs of yellow eyes peering at them, but suddenly the bobsled dropped, seemingly straight down, and a second later emerged into the light again.

Sata screamed, wondering for a moment if she could stop the ride to go back and get her stomach. A moment later she laughed at herself.

That same plunge in the darkness made Boro completely sure he was about to die, if not on this stretch of track, then the next. Time slowed for him, and suddenly he was back on a medieval cattle ranch, at about age five, trying desperately to make a huge long-horned cow go where he wanted it to go, and feeling sure he was about to die. Moments later he was on the slave auction block, six or seven years later, fearing his next master would beat him to death for being too clumsy. Next, guards surrounded him and his friends and teacher, the high priest wore an evil grin, and Boro *knew* the dungeon was next. Finally, he was fully prepared to die on an icy planet, but had lived to see the stars again.

After all that, he suddenly realized why he had been able to surrender to death gracefully during the Great Transformation on Satamia Star Station. Although he certainly *preferred* to live, no fear of dying remained in his heart. So if he was going to die on the next stretch of Ice Mountain Bobsled track, and couldn't do anything about it, he might as well enjoy it.

Sata heard his howl of excitement, right behind her, and knew her friend had just found a new depth of joy inside himself. She added her own shriek as daylight and darkness flashed around them three more times, then suddenly water was spraying up all around and they were pressed forward into their inertia straps.

*

Boro felt his heart pounding in his chest, and was dimly aware that the bobsled hadn't come to a complete stop in the water, but had slowed just enough to bring it out of the pond and back to the boarding station with a gentle bump into the line of cars on the track.

Sata felt Boro's arms surround and hold her tightly. She closed her eyes, smiled, and listened to her own heart pounding.

Neither was aware of the passage of time, but a few minutes later they were brought back to the present by the bump of another bobsled car into theirs from behind.

"Bok!" exclaimed an avian voice who had also just had the ride of her life.

* * *

Chapter 23: The Monkey-Mammal Cage

The next day, the elderly pair of original station hosts were anxious to continue their story.

"Long before we could figure out the water system, or start on the animal-proof fence, we had to get familiar with our neighborhood," Jimox explained.

Teina grinned with her few remaining teeth. "The Cage."

Jimox nodded and cleared his throat.

* * *

About a month after arriving in Similand, Jimox and Teina had found the master keys, unlocked everything, and knew what supplies were available. Food that needed to be kept cold with electricity, and hadn't been for the last seven years, had no value. Every few days, they worked up the courage to clean out another refrigerator or freezer. A fair amount of edibles remained, but many things were missing. No one had come to Similand to buy basic groceries, hardware, or work clothes, so the pair of monkey mammals was forced to explore the city around them.

They found everything they could possibly want, stacked on store shelves waiting for them, often enough untouched by vermin. But thousands, maybe millions of wild dogs roamed the city constantly.

Three times they watched, safely perched in trees or on stone walls, as a pack of hungry canines, unable to get fresh monkey-mammal meat, rummaged through the cart of supplies Jimox and Teina had just spent all day gathering, spoiling most things. Sometimes they could shoot one or two, but the nearest safe place was often too far for accurate pistol shots. Even if their aim was good, the carcass just attracted more dogs.

Every time it happened, Jimox fussed and fumed for several days. Teina directed his frustration into helping her clean out old refrigerators and freezers.

One day they were exploring the Similand service area when they came upon a large animal cage on wheels, big enough for a lion or two. Jimox' face lit up, and he quickly determined that it rolled easily on rubber tires. "It'll protect our stuff from the dogs!"

Teina was just as happy with the find, and helped Jimox pump up the tires, then fit pieces of plywood to the insides of the bars, from the floor to about halfway up, so that nothing could even *drool* on their supplies.

Twice it worked as intended. The pair watched from a balcony or a rooftop as dogs tried desperately to get at the food within, but eventually had to give up and look elsewhere. Other dogs, and starvation itself, were always close.

The third time was different.

The mobile cage was half-full of food, candles, and batteries, when a group of dogs appeared in front of them, and another behind. Both monkey mammals scanned for a safe place. Everything was too far. Jimox pulled out his pistol, ready to make a stand.

"Too many!" Teina shrieked. "Inside the cage!"

Jimox blinked a couple of times, saw the dogs approaching fast, and knew in his heart that Teina was right. He scampered after her onto the supplies inside, and she pulled the cage door closed just as the first dogs arrived.

While the attackers fruitlessly tried to jump high enough to see the tasty morsels within, Jimox and Teina slowly relaxed and got as comfortable as they could.

"I'm sitting on a bag of corn meal," Jimox said with a smile. "How about you?"

She looked down. "A deep-cycle battery!"

They both laughed heartily as wild dogs continued to snap and growl all around them.

An hour later, they were able to continue their journey homeward.

*   *   *

Teina laughed so hard from the memory that she almost cried.

Eventually, she settled down enough to speak. "The next time we went scrounging, Jimox had cut a hole in the wooden roof of the cage, just big enough to climb up through, and I had put a little tent up there, complete with sleeping bags, books to read, and some emergency supplies."

"We called it our Monkey-Mammal Cage, and it became more and more important as the years passed, and we had to go farther and farther from Similand for supplies."

* * *

Chapter 24: Critter-Proof

"*Now* can we tell them about your fantastic water system?" Jimox asked his beloved partner, tail wrapped all the way around her.

"No! They have to hear about the wonderful animal-proof fence you made, and how we got the dogs out of Similand!"

Jimox squirmed with embarrassment, but saw the sparkles of pride in Teina's old eyes, so he reluctantly took a deep breath.

"We settled into a routine that lasted for almost two years — three days a week on each project, the extra day for scrounging and exploring. As we got closer and closer to getting the fence done, we were both dreading the final step — killing all the dogs in Similand — because neither one of us actually *liked* killing anything. There were about a dozen who lived here all the time, and another half-dozen who just visited. We were starting to give them names . . ."

* * *

About a week after deciding to make the fence around Similand completely dog-proof, Jimox and Teina set out in the cool air of early morning with a pad of paper, a hundred-foot tape measure, sun hats on their heads, and pistols in their holsters.

"Main exit," Jimox dictated, "sixteen feet wide, needs wire along the bottom. Small dogs can squeeze under."

Teina wrote with her simple printing, glancing up often to help keep watch. "Got it. But it's high enough, right?"

"Yeah. I've never seen a dog who could jump over an eight-foot fence, but this stretch of four-foot behind the ticket booths has to be improved."

They worked in silence with the tape measure, both looking around often.

"Seventy-five feet," Jimox announced.

"Got it."

"Then comes this section, all the way to the west service entrance, where they can dig under, and *have* in several places."

The pair walked in silence as Jimox paced off the distance.

"A hundred and five paces, needs railroad ties, concrete blocks, whatever."

"And has five crawl-holes already. Got it."

They both stood gazing at the service entrance to Machineland. Even horses could easily get through.

"This is the worst part. I'm gonna look for a couple of wide gates we can put in, attach them to the lamp posts on each side. Forty-six feet across, guard house covers the middle four feet."

"Got it. Two big mutts coming down the street!"

"Guard house!"

The pair of monkey mammals watched as the dogs sniffed around, sensing something to eat, but unable to find it.

*

Months later, the pair clung to the top of a ladder as three dogs fought over the right to smell, chew, and mark the fencing tools and supplies on the ground.

"No, not my wire cutters!" Jimox lamented. "I hate dog piss on my wire cutters."

Teina laughed so hard she almost fell off the ladder. "That's old Blackie! He marks *everything!*"

Jimox held onto her as she wobbled. "Be careful, or he'll be marking *you!*"

"Sorry, but you have to admit, it was funny!" she responded, still chuckling. Then she looked down again. "Oh, no, don't you dare steal my tape measure, Slinky!"

It was Jimox' turn to laugh, but he kept a strong arm on the fence on one side, and around Teina on the other.

All the dogs ran off behind Slinky.

"Shall we take a break?" Jimox proposed. "Wash the wire cutters and get another tape measure? We've got plenty."

Teina pouted. "I suppose."

A moment later she forced out a smile.

*

Finally the day arrived when the pair of brown monkey mammals pushed a cart loaded with railroad ties along the sidewalk, just outside the theme park, to fill the last three places where dogs could dig under the fence.

"This is kinda scary," Teina admitted as she kept watch while Jimox, with leather gloves, worked each railroad tie into place. He couldn't carry the heavy tar-soaked timbers, but could lift one end and pivot them a little, sometimes gaining just a few inches at a time. Finally, three railroad ties filled the gap between the sidewalk and the fence.

"If this works," the nineteen-year-old boy began as they pushed the cart to the next hole, "it'll be the first time since . . . we were kids . . . that we could go outside without deadly dangers all around us."

"Yeah," the fifteen-year-old girl agreed, "it'll be the first time we could just . . . play!"

They both laughed out loud at the thought as they came to the next canine crawl-hole.

Teina checked the cylinder of her pistol as Jimox worked. "But I think we should still carry guns."

Jimox dropped a railroad tie into place. "Yeah. There's too much fence for us to patrol it constantly. Things will get in sometimes."

The cart now much lighter, they moved to the last weak place in the fence surrounding their precious Similand.

As Jimox worked the final timber into place, then jumped up and down on it to make sure it was solid, Teina frowned. "The next thing we have to do is gonna be hard."

Jimox was silent as he tossed his gloves into the tool box on the cart. "What in our lives has ever been easy, since . . ."

"Burning Day," she finished the thought.

The front entrance was closest, so they pushed the cart in that direction. The entrance turnstiles were now completely covered by wire fencing, well-attached to poles and pinned to the ground with heavy concrete blocks. Teina maneuvered the cart toward the amusement park's main exit, a wide gate that was easy to swing open. The latch had been placed high enough to be unreachable by children . . . and dogs.

But before she could even reach for the latch, a shimmering golden glow suddenly got in her face and began scolding with a faint but determined voice.

"Giona! What is it?"

Jimox had been checking the turnstile fencing and keeping watch. "This must be important. We haven't seen her in *months!*"

Try as they might, neither monkey mammals could understand what the little spirit was trying to tell them. A few words like "dogs" and "danger" came through, almost more as a feeling in their bones than audible words. But they couldn't deny that the ghost clearly did not want them to go through that gate.

Jimox looked around. "Ladder up to the Kid's Motorway? We can see what's going on from there."

Teina nodded, but took a moment to put their tool box onto an old drinking fountain where it would be safe.

Jimox smiled.

*

Once they climbed onto the elevated miniature motorway, both pulled out their pistols. They knew dogs rarely got onto it, but *could* at each station, if determined enough.

A short walk back toward the main entrance allowed the pair to see Olde Towne, and they immediately understood what Giona was trying to tell them.

The usual dozen or so resident dogs, the visitors Jimox and Teina recognized, and several more they didn't, were all going crazy. They madly tore at whatever they could get their teeth around — posts, flower pots, signs, and each other.

Teina and Jimox watched with wide eyes from the relative safety of the motorway as the frenzy continued, sometimes surging to the front gate, and sometimes vanishing into one of the streets of Olde Towne. But after a few minutes, the dogs returned, all together, and each time they seemed wilder and more frustrated.

"I think ..." Jimox began, "they're gone just long enough each time to check one of the crawl-holes we closed up yesterday or today."

Teina nodded. "They're more dangerous than ever like this, acting like one big pack."

Jimox was silent for a minute as he watched the chaos below. "I . . . don't want to kill them."

Teina looked at him. "It's them or us . . . or we can give up Similand and go live in the big old train station."

Jimox frowned. "I didn't mean *that*. I mean I want to let them out. And I think I know a way."

*

Jimox shared his plan as they climbed back down the ladder.

Teina grinned and nodded.

A fast walk completely around the outside of Similand took nearly half an hour, but it was necessary for the plan to work. They opened the Machineland service gate on the west side, the Castleland employee's entrance on the north, the Forestland emergency exit on the east, and finally the main exit that Giona had forbidden them to use. This time, she seemed to understand their intentions, and didn't mind.

After climbing back up the ladder to the Kid's Motorway, they crept to their dwelling in the Olde Towne station and filled their pockets with boxes of bullets.

The only dangerous part of the plan was the dash across open ground from the nearest motorway station to the World Tree, about a hundred meters during which the wild dogs could get them. They waited until the pack surged toward Machineland, then ran.

The frenzied dogs were soon back, just as Jimox and Teina ascended the first ladder into the lower branches of the huge artificial tree. Part of the pack dashed into Forestland, a few went toward Olde Towne.

Jimox looked around. An old sign dangling by one corner caught his eye, so he yanked until it came loose. Teina opened boxes of ammunition.

He held the sign like a shield, with his pistol in front, and looked back at Teina.

She nodded.

Jimox fired all six bullets into the air, avoiding the direction of any glass windows.

Even though the sign had directed most of the sound away from them, still their ears rang, so they didn't attempt any further communication. He handed the sign to her, and she unloaded her pistol in a different direction while he reloaded.

They went back and forth, directing a blast of deafening noise toward each of the lands of the theme park, three times for each land.

Teina saved just enough bullets for one final reload, then raised her hand.

They listened, and couldn't hear a thing.

Jimox said something, and Teina frowned.

She spoke, and he was clueless.

They both laughed, but as far as they could tell, both of them were laughing silently.

* * *

"Luckily, our deafness only lasted about an hour," Teina reassured her worried listeners, then paused to cough deeply.

"But in that hour," Jimox took over, "we had to close all four gates, without being able to hear each other, *or* any approaching dangers."

"But it worked, and I was very proud of Jimox!" she said, her tail wrapped around him. "Only two dogs remained in Similand that we had to get rid of the old-fashioned way."

* * *

Chapter 25: No Equipment Needed

Another day came when the elderly couple was not up to telling stories, so all the invited guests scattered to join the hundreds of other visitors who were busy enjoying the attractions of Siminia Three Planet Station.

Rini smiled, seeing their three passengers, monkey mammal, bird, and snake, head off side-by-side to explore the theme park.

"They're getting to be fast friends," Mati observed.

"Yeah. Ashley's a little embarrassed by it, but all three of them love it when they don't have to work on their essays so they can go off together."

"Kolarrr'ka's little harem."

Rini laughed. "I don't know about *that!*"

Mati joined him in laughter.

"What do you want to do?" Rini asked to change the subject.

"Um ... something easy. That one where we needed gloves and ropes took more energy than I have today."

Rini was content. He would have been happy sweeping floors with his beloved Mati.

*

They wandered the streets and alleys of Olde Towne, peeking into shops where the remaining goods were now museum pieces. Restaurants had all the original furnishings and decorations, but the only food was from a Nebador nutrition cabinet. Theaters displayed the original plastic projection films on reels, brittle with age, but the show could still be watched on a Nebador display screen.

At the very end of a tiny alley, something grabbed Mati's interest and almost pulled her in against her will. While she grinned with excitement, one foot already in the door, Rini took the time to read the sign. *"Journey Through Time. Completely restored by Nebador technicians. No dangers. No special equipment needed."*

He looked at her and nodded.

✳

The lobby was once a maze of ropes to keep hundreds of monkey mammals occupied while the attraction within struggled to keep up with their numbers. Now, the ropes had been rearranged so a large equine or fanator could walk right in.

The journey began high in the shadowy branches of a primeval jungle. A mixture of detailed sculpture, subtle lighting, painted backgrounds, and moving projections brought the scenes to life. The wild creatures of the air and the denizens of the forest floor lurked everywhere, calling to each other in harsh voices, and often showing long, sharp teeth. They acted, until the very last moment, as if whatever walked on the carpeted path would be their next meal, bones and all. An emergency exit allowed the faint-of-heart to leave the attraction early.

Mati grinned at Rini. *"This is fun!"*

Soon a strong monkey mammal with golden-brown fur appeared in the trees. Lightning struck one tree, and he bravely grabbed a burning branch, then swung through the forest with his torch, sending all the dangerous animals screaming for their lives.

Mati was wide-eyed.

Rini just smiled.

The forest became an idyllic paradise of deer and rabbits nibbling grass. Furry monkey mammals tended orderly gardens, built cozy thatched cottages, and played in the forest with the harmless wild creatures.

"That is so wonderful!" Mati declared. "I wish *our* kingdom could have been like that."

Rini raised his eyebrows.

The ground shook and miniature volcanoes spewed simulated molten rock. Determined monkey mammals used tame elephants and other large beasts to drag huge blocks of stone to channel the lava. Power plants sprang up to turn the heat into electricity.

Mati grinned. "See what people can do when they work together instead of buying and selling each other as slaves?"

Rini knew it wasn't meant to be a question, but he nodded anyway.

Teams of happy craftsmen began building modern cities that glowed with lights and buzzed with trains and cars. Everywhere, monkey mammals shook hands and worked together to build bridges, schools, libraries, and Similand itself.

"Wow," Mati breathed. "No slavery, no crime, no poverty. Look, even the mayor's helping to build a school, and all the monkey-mammal children with different fur colors are playing together nicely!"

Rini smiled, completely happy with the idea.

Finally, a simple rocket blasted off, carrying two brave monkey mammals toward the stars. The lighted scenes and projections ended, and a large display room contained all the great discoveries of Siminia Three science and technology, in glass cases, so Similand guests could continue to feel pride in the accomplishments of their ancestors throughout the ages.

After silently wandering around the display room for a quarter hour, Mati started to frown.

Rini noticed and looked at her.

"Something's wrong," Mati eventually said.

Rini nodded slightly, but didn't say anything.

"If everything was so wonderful, how did they get to . . . where they were when Jimox and Teina were young, making biological weapons of mass destruction in secret laboratories?"

Rini cracked a slight smile, but remained silent.

"If they were making weapons, there must have been a war. If there was a war, they couldn't have been so good at getting along."

Rini nodded slowly.

Suddenly Mati dashed back into the attraction. The control systems didn't seem to care which direction a visitor went. They sensed her presence, and activated the lights and projections as she entered each area.

Mati gazed at the pastoral scene of people gardening and children playing with wild animals. Rini joined her.

After a minute of staring with wrinkled brow, she sighed. "Something's missing here. I learned in Psychic Development that people don't just become all goodie-goodie when they no longer have to fight to survive. If they're smart, they direct those instincts into sports and other stuff."

"Makes sense," Rini said.

Mati strode farther back through the attraction, stopping at the primeval jungle where a monkey mammal first tamed fire. "If this is even *partly* true . . ."

She dashed forward in time again, stopping at the lava channels. "Okay, the taming-fire theme comes up twice. I have no problem with that."

She returned to the pastoral scene. "But I happen to know, from universe history classes, that people don't subdue all the dangerous wild animals without going through a *long* period — usually thousands of years — when they use and abuse *everything*, including the most harmless of animals, and including *themselves*."

"Like with slavery," Rini whispered.

"Yeah! And that's . . . totally missing."

Rini let a long moment pass. "Do you think . . ."

She looked at him as he searched for the right words.

". . . they left something out of the display, or just never actually got to, you know, where they wanted to be in the development of their civilization?"

As Mati thought about his question, she walked backward and forward through the entire attraction again. Rini stayed at her side. She stopped at the last scene, a modern city buzzing with happy, peaceful citizens.

"They got there *technologically* — you know, buildings, electricity, trains, cars, and all that. We've seen the ruins, museum pieces, and a few preserved buildings. That part of the display is true enough."

"But . . ." Rini prompted softly.

Mati re-entered the display room. "There's nothing here about weapons or wars, especially biological weapons. They didn't get to where they wanted to be *in their hearts*. They were good at telling stories, like all sapient peoples, so they told themselves stories about who they wanted to be . . . and that's what they put in this whole attraction. That's *all* they put in it."

After a long moment, Rini said, "I agree."

*

After a few more minutes wandering around the display room, Mati and Rini stepped through the exit door and emerged into the sunshine. One more Nebador sign faced them.

"*The scenes you just witnessed are not historically accurate,*" Rini read. "*They depict the myths that the former civilization liked to remember, and teach to their children. In many cases, they did not even record the actual, often embarrassing, events of their history.*"

"Thought so," Mati said.

*   *   *

Chapter 26: Water, Water Everywhere

Jimox and Teina were still shivering slightly from the morning coolness, so they selected a bench in the warm morning sun. "*Now* can we tell them about your fantastic water system?"

She kissed him. "Okay."

"Back when I was still scratching my head over how to fix the fence, Teina quickly figured out the water pipes inside Similand. But she just didn't have much water to work with . . ."

* * *

Morning sun streamed through the windows of the Kid's Motorway station, so Jimox sat up and stretched his brown furry arms. Teina was still in dreamland, so he looked over the shelves of food and supplies all around him, brimming with everything that had survived the seven or more years since they were packaged.

A few minutes later, Teina stirred, heard the little gas camp stove hissing, and turned over. "What'cha making?"

"Oatmeal with raisins and brown sugar."

"Mmmm! Count me in!" she said, sitting up. "What are we doing today?"

"Up to you. It's a water-project day. Besides, I can't do any more on the fence until we get more wire. It's on the scrounging list."

"Hmmm . . ." she began, stretching and pulling on clothes. "I guess we know everything there is to know about the pipes and valves in Similand. We have to find that water company office and figure out where the water's coming from."

"Bikes and day packs?"

"Yeah, and flashlights. All your *can openers*, of course."

Jimox smiled and glanced at his leather bag of pry bars and bolt cutters. "Oatmeal's ready."

*

As always, they walked the outside of the concrete building to see if anything had found a way in, and might be waiting for them inside. Finding the building secure, they looked for an entry point that would allow them to close it again. Jimox settled on a metal loading-ramp door, and went to work.

An alarm screamed at them, until its old batteries died about twenty seconds later. In that time it tried desperately to call the police, but couldn't get a dial tone.

"The ghost of a machine," Jimox mused, "trying to do its job one last time."

Teina blinked. "A little sad. Let's unlock the front door and bring the bikes in."

*

Light streamed in through the glass doors of the carpeted front lobby, illuminating the vending machines and a three-D model of the entire water system. Shoulder to shoulder, they studied it.

"Doesn't tell us much more than we already know," Teina concluded. "I can't tell which of the three reservoirs in the hills is ours. I'm gonna have to find real maps and charts."

"Let me know if I can do anything. In the meantime, I'll harvest the vending machines."

The thirteen-year-old monkey mammal girl began walking the corridors, looking for the map room.

*

An hour later, she spread out four huge charts on the carpet. Jimox placed drink cans on the corners so they wouldn't roll back up, and Teina crouched on the floor and peered at them. "Okay, now we've got every pipe and valve. Here's Similand, with a big water main going in. Would you grab the blue highlighter and follow that pipe?"

"Sure."

She moved to a different chart. "Now I can see the big pipes coming from the dams. This one goes off south, so it can't be ours. It has to be one of these two."

Jimox looked up. "Okay, I came to the edge of my chart. What about the dam closest to Similand?"

"That's just emergency overflow from this one, and doesn't connect to the water system. Would you trace the pipe from the middle reservoir? Orange, please."

Jimox switched markers and began coloring.

"Yeah. Okay, I see how these charts match up."

"Wrong reservoir again," Jimox announced. "It just turned and went straight north."

Teina looked. "Okay, I'll color this pipe yellow, you continue the Similand pipe onto this chart, and we'll see what happens."

Their lines got closer and closer, until they came together at the matching edges of two charts. They looked at each other. Jimox suddenly felt a burst of courage, leaned forward, and kissed Teina on the cheek."

"Why did you do that?" she asked with a trembling voice.

"Because I have the most wonderful friend that anyone could ever want."

She blushed and blinked. "Okay ... um ... it looks like our water is coming from Pine Canyon."

Jimox grabbed his day pack, unfolded a street map, and looked at the roads between the water company office and the reservoir. "About an hour and a half from here. We could go today, if you want."

✳

An hour and a half of pedaling brought them to the lower end of a dirt road that wound steeply up into the hills. Another hour of pushing their bicycles revealed the bottom of the dam, and a water filtration plant.

Inside the building, plenty of water was flowing into the concrete filter tanks, but the sand was so caked with algae that the water just sheeted across to the overflow channel.

Teina frowned. "I'm not exactly sure how this is supposed to work, but it obviously isn't."

Jimox nodded. "Sorry about my bad time estimates."

She kissed him on the cheek. "Let's see what we can see at the top."

✳

Half an hour later, the top of the dam spread across the canyon to their right. Ahead of them, if they looked down, a few hundred yards of stagnant green water and weeds sat in the bottom of the reservoir, with a stream feeding it at the far end.

"Eeew," Teina remarked.

Jimox frowned. "I'm glad we haven't been drinking from our little trickle in Forestland."

She nodded, then looked at the sun, already getting low. "We need a couple of days to figure this out."

They both looked around, and quickly spotted the caretaker's house, nearly hidden in a cluster of trees. Luckily, he hadn't been home on Burning Day.

✳ ✳ ✳

"You were just thirteen," Mati said, looking at Teina with an understanding smile, "same as me when I became a response-ship pilot."

Teina grinned back. "For the next year and a half ..." She stopped when her breath gave out, and looked at Jimox.

"For the next year and a half, we had to find and close about a thousand valves, all going to neighborhoods with burned houses where the water was just leaking into the ground. We opened man hole covers and crept into dark tunnels, pried locks off little concrete buildings covered with stickers, and tried not to turn off the water going to Similand."

"We accidentally did, about five times!" Teina added.

Jimox put his arm around her. "Slowly, the water pressure here came up. Today, all the ponds are full, and the fountains, waterfalls, and streams are flowing with fresh water, day and night. There's drinking water and wash water, and it all comes from the same reservoir!"

"And the filter works!" Teina added, then started coughing.

"She worked on that for a whole day every time we went to the dam, which was about once a month. She was as determined as I was about the fence, and made several improvements in the design."

"You're embarrassing me. As soon as I raked off the algae, it started working. Now there's a specialist from Nebador who keeps it in good shape." She paused to cough. "But we wanted to tell them how we hooked up with Nebador."

Jimox took on a stern expression. "Not until we tell them how we came to live in Fairy Castle."

Teina grinned. "You're right. Our story wouldn't be complete without *that.*"

✳ ✳ ✳

Chapter 27: Rini's Investigation

Rini had been in a very thoughtful mood ever since he and Mati explored *Journey Through Time*. So at the lunch break, and again that evening, he declared that he needed to spend time in some museums. Mati had already had her fill of museums, so she and Sata dashed off toward Machineland.

Rini was glad he was alone. He wasn't exactly sure what he was looking for, and had a hunch it might take a while to find.

Siminia Three Planet Station and its retreats contained dozens of museums, as they were now the only buildings of the old civilization that were maintained. The retreats, like Paradise Lodge, held a few paintings and sculptures for decoration, Rini knew, but most of the museum pieces were right here.

The first four museums, each of which took him more than an hour to browse, did not get him any closer to his goal. The paintings, sculptures, and books were all very beautiful, certainly worthy of preservation, and made him sad to think that the civilization that created them was gone. But they didn't shed light on the big question he had been pondering ever since *Journey Through Time*.

He exited the last museum on a tiny side street of Olde Towne, and happened to glance toward the end of the narrow alley. Beside a large trash can, he spotted a small door with an even smaller sign beside it. His curiosity piqued, he approached.

Below the original lettering in the dead language now spoken by only two elderly people, someone had inscribed a translation in the language of Nebador.

"Famous Movie Sets," Rini muttered to himself.

He pushed on the door. Its rusty hinges complained, but allowed him to enter.

*

With his bracelet light, Rini peered at arrangements of fancy furniture, re-creations of famous rooms in old-fashioned palaces and modern offices, and laboratories where scientists discovered the secrets of nature.

Something creepy about most of the laboratories caused Rini to raise his eyebrows.

He continued deeper into the dark building and discovered more and more movie sets that involved glass tubing and flasks, strange electrical panels with huge switches, and beds where a monkey mammal could be strapped down.

Rini swallowed.

Occasionally he came upon the plush office of a famous leader, or the polished wooden bar from an old drinking saloon, but soon another laboratory would appear, even more gruesome than the last. Cages held plastic animals, fear showing in their painted eyes. In one lab, a mock-up of a full-size monkey mammal was strapped down, tubes in its arms and electrodes on its head. Its artificial eyes, too, were wide with fear.

Rini shivered and felt his stomach churn.

*

After two hours in *Famous Movie Sets*, Rini took a deep breath. He felt sure he was getting closer to what he was looking for, but needed to continue following the clues. Unfortunately, all the signs inside this museum were only in the language of the dead civilization.

After another moment of thought, he dashed back through the entire building, taking a photograph of each laboratory set with his bracelet, making sure to include the sign that revealed the name of the movie.

*

Evening was deepening into night as Rini stepped into the control room in the Fairy Castle tower. Rrr'tana the station host was in the lounge area teaching a pair of reptilian assistants the landing procedures for arriving ships. A small ursine was at the monitor desk scanning visual scenes from around the planet station. Another stood at one of the eight windows, the one that looked out over Machineland.

Rini found a seat in a corner and waited until Rrr'tana was free. A while later the bird sent his new helpers out to observe fully-trained assistant hosts in the process of landing a large ship. Finally the host looked at the freckled lad and bowed.

"Do you know the old language of Siminia Three?" Rini asked, standing up.

"I can read it, bok, but only Jimox and Teina can speak it properly."

Rini touched some keys on his bracelet to transfer the images to a monitor. "I'd like to watch as many of these videos as I can."

Rrr'tana nodded. "We probably have them. I need to observe this landing, then I'll transfer them to Manessa."

"Thank you!" Rini said as he bowed to the station host.

Rrr'tana stepped to a window as Rini bounded down the steps to see what

Mati was doing.

✳

After rowing around Forestland Lake by lantern light with Mati, dancing under the World Tree to some recorded music from the former civilization with Mati, Sata, and Ashley, and finally whizzing down Ice Mountain in a bobsled with Boro, Rini arrived back at the Manessa Kwi feeling quite ready for bed.

"I have the twenty-one videos you requested," the ship informed him.

After kissing Mati good-night, Rini couldn't resist the temptation to creep back up to the passenger area.

None of the movies had been translated into the language of Nebador, but Rini wasn't worried. He wasn't looking for factual information. He wanted to feel, with his heart, if maybe the monkey mammals of Siminia Three had created the disease that destroyed their civilization in fulfillment of some longing in their collective subconscious.

✳

As the third video was ending, Rini glanced at the open hatch and noticed that dawn light was in the sky.

A few minutes later, Mati came up and snuggled into the passenger seat with him. "Did you find what you were looking for?"

Rini nodded.

✳   ✳   ✳

Chapter 28: Moving Day

A new day dawned bright and clear, so after a few minutes in the morning sunshine, Jimox and Teina moved into the shade of one of the large Castleland trees.

"Until we got that fence done, we had just been hiding in the Olde Towne Kid's Motorway station, coming out to creep around and work on our projects quickly before anything tried to eat us."

Teina chuckled.

"We shot the last two wild dogs, kept creeping around for another week, then realized that we had actually done it — we had actually cleaned out the only dangerous animals in Similand."

Kibi clapped, and the other listeners joined her.

Teina grinned. "There were cats and raccoons," she admitted, "opossums, rats, and mice, but none of them were up to feasting on full-grown monkey mammals."

Jimox smiled. "And once we cleaned out all the spoiled and unprotected food, most of the rats and mice vanished, too."

"For a while," Teina continued, "we didn't know what to do. We were almost in shock. We could actually, for the first time, just *live*, but it had been so long that we had almost forgotten how!"

Everyone laughed or fluffed up their feathers.

"But as the days passed, and we became more and more sure that nothing dangerous remained in Similand, or could get back in, we started having some ideas . . ."

✳ ✳ ✳

In a red child's wagon, a deep-cycle battery powered a sine-wave inverter, and a cord snaked across the Forestland plaza to where Teina swung an electric weed trimmer back and forth.

Jimox swept where Teina had already finished. Occasionally he glanced up and scanned the plaza for dogs, but three months without an intruder, and a few adjustments to the animal-proof fence, had made them feel quite safe.

Coming to the end of a long seam in the pavement, and the meter-high weeds that had called it home, she released the trigger and walked back to the wagon. "Down to twelve volts."

"Good time to put it on the solar panel," Jimox replied. "Lunch after I finish sweeping?"

"Yeah," she said, looking up at the sky. "Sun's gonna break through the clouds soon. Any chance we can try the shower today?"

"I think so, if I got all the right parts at the hardware store yesterday."

They worked in silence for a few minutes, Teina coiling her cord and Jimox scooping the trimmings into a wheeled trash barrel. Then they held tails as she pulled the wagon and he rolled the barrel toward the front of Similand.

But as soon as they emerged from Forestland, and arrived at the wide pathway that encircled the World Tree, they both came to a sudden stop and stared at the ground.

"*What* is our two-quart sauce pan doing on the ground, right there?" Teina asked, looking at her partner with a smile.

Jimox didn't answer, but quickly stepped to the wagon and pulled a pistol from a holster.

Seeing his serious reaction, Teina scanned in all directions. "I take it . . . you didn't leave it there."

"No," he replied, joining her in scanning. "I've never taken it out of the motorway station."

Teina swallowed. "Me neither."

Convinced that no danger was close, Jimox knelt down to examine the evidence. "Weird. No slobber, no teeth marks on the handle. It's completely clean and undamaged."

"High Alert until we check the fence," Teina asserted.

Jimox nodded, then put the sauce pan into the wagon.

✳

On the short walk back to their dwelling in Olde Towne, they found three more items that neither of them had left, nor had any reason to bring outside.

They were especially confused when they came to a plastic bag of dried meat, with no signs of any attempt to open it.

Their home was secure, with no evidence that anything had broken in. But they could think of a dozen thing that were missing.

After a quick lunch eaten in tense silence, both wore double pistol belts as they stepped through the main exit gate to walk the outside perimeter of their sanctuary.

*

No breach in the fence, of any kind, was found.

For the next hour, they looked for clues in and around the motorway station, on the streets of Olde Towne, and in the plazas and pathways of Forestland, Castleland, and Machineland.

Nothing revealed itself.

They even climbed some of the ladders of the World Tree, and slid down the slides. Nothing.

Jimox took a slow breath as he looked around. "There's no way we can check every nook and cranny in Similand."

Teina sighed. "As much as I don't like this idea . . . I guess we just have to wait for . . . whatever it is . . . to show itself."

Jimox nodded. "But we stay on High Alert."

"Agreed."

*

High Alert meant that only one of them could work, just as if they were outside the animal-proof fence. After getting the plumbing cart from its garage on the service street of Olde Towne, Teina rode, constantly scanning, while Jimox pushed.

At their destination, a small building with a flat roof exposed to the sun, Teina climbed the ladder and sprayed black paint onto the long pipe they had already installed that snaked back and forth all over the roof. Jimox paced with pistols handy and a frown on his face.

Once she came down, Jimox worked with pipe fittings and wrenches while Teina patrolled, and a couple of hours later, the mixing valve was installed and the project ready to be tested.

They looked at each other.

"This was supposed to be a *fun* addition to a *safe* and *secure* Similand," Jimox said with frustration.

Teina put an arm around him. "Whatever we're dealing with — I'm guessing raccoon — I don't think we should let it stop us from having fun. We're almost positive it's not a dog. That's the only thing we have to worry about, except maybe a lion or tiger from the zoo."

Jimox smiled. "Nothing that big could have gotten into the motorway station. I'll go with your raccoon theory. Okay, I'm on watch, you're testing this contraption."

Teina opened the main valve a little, and heard water flow up the pipe toward the roof. She waited, watching the shower head, while Jimox tried not to.

A minute later, steam came hissing out of the shower head. "Too hot," Teina declared.

"Increase the flow," Jimox counseled.

Soon they had liquid water — scalding hot, but at least liquid. Once the flow to the roof pipe was at maximum, and the water was still too hot, Teina started adjusting the cold side of the mixing valve. "Ahhh! I'm on watch, you get first shower!"

Jimox was nervous at first, but soon relaxed into the first hot shower he had had in a decade.

*

When they finally got home at close to sunset, both their mouths fell open. Most of their belongings and supplies were gone, and the few that remained were scattered around the room as if a tornado had come through.

* * *

"I would have been scared," Sata admitted.

"Angry," Mati added.

"Curious," Rini suggested.

"Worried," Ashley said.

"We were all those things!" Teina shared, then coughed and nearly turned blue.

Jimox stroked her ragged white fur until she relaxed. "Luckily, our bed was still there. But we didn't get much sleep that night."

With wide eyes, Kibi nodded. "I can understand why!"

* * *

As soon as first light crept into the sky, both young monkey mammals were wide awake. A package of dried fruit — somehow missed by the unknown invaders — served as breakfast.

Teina was not in a good mood. "We have to start all over, scrounge up food, cooking stuff, tools . . . everything!"

Jimox scooted close and surrounded her with his arms and tail. "I'm frustrated too. Let's take it a step at a time. Maybe morning light will give us a clue about where our stuff is."

"In some stupid *coon's* nest somewhere! The only reason they left us breakfast was they couldn't carry it all!"

Their patience was sorely tested waiting for sunrise, but a package of old cookies from Jimox' day pack helped pass the time. While they nibbled in silence, pistols were checked and extra ammunition pocketed.

In the clear light of day, clues were not hard to find. Packages of food, some already pecked open by birds, had been dropped along two streets of Olde Towne, and around the World Tree.

Jimox knelt down. "Pecking, but no teeth marks, not even little sharp teeth like a raccoon."

Teina frowned.

They continued to follow the evidence. It led them directly to Castleland.

At first, the trail seemed to go everywhere at once in the part of Similand dedicated to the age of glory and battle. With guns drawn, they poked their heads into several rides and walk-through attractions, but in each case, the trail went cold. They fared no better in the snack bars, or the Castle Kitchen itself.

That left the three castles.

A package of crackers lay on the drawbridge to the Knight's Castle, and a bird flew off as they approached, but they found nothing more, even after taking the entire walk-through route that allowed them to peek into every room.

They stood in the plaza and looked at the two remaining options. Three or four items could be seen on the approaches to both the Fairy Castle and the Witch's Castle.

"Your choice," Jimox said, spinning the cylinder of his pistol.

"I don't care. Fairy."

They paused briefly at each item, and again saw no evidence of dogs or raccoons.

In the Party Room, among all the dishes and decorations, they spotted their bag of pry bars and bolt cutters. Jimox frowned. "No bird, smaller than an eagle, could carry *that*."

The Magic Room contained every color of fairy dust, gemstones galore, racks of magic wands, and their gas camp stove. "Not even an eagle could have carried that here!" Teina declared with a very puzzled expression, looking it over. "And what animal would set it up, on its legs, with the gas bottle beside it, all neat and tidy, and the gas hose not even twisted? That's even hard for *me!*"

Jimox chuckled. "So . . . the raccoon theory is in question . . ."

"Serious question!"

Next on the walk-through route, they arrived at the Fairy King and Queen's Chamber.

Most of their belongings could be seen, scattered around the room. Some were on tables, a few on shelves, but many still on the floor. Even as the pair looked on, two or three items floated through the air and landed on a table or shelf. Sometimes they remained, but if they didn't fit, they rose back into the air and floated somewhere else.

Jimox and Teina stood with their mouths hanging open.

✳ ✳ ✳

The elderly monkey mammals grinned at their listeners.

"Ghossstsss!" T'sss'lisss whispered.

Teina nodded. "But then something happened that changed *everything!*"

✳ ✳ ✳

More of their possessions floated in through a window as the young pair stood gazing at the strange scene before them. Invisible forces seemed to be trying to organize it all, just as it had been at the Kid's Motorway station.

Regaining her wits, Teina recognized a small golden glow. "Giona!"

The little ghost, who had traveled with them ever since Paradise Lodge, zoomed over.

"What's going on?" Teina asked pointedly.

Giona made a tiny sound that might have been a giggle, then said two words clearly. "Stay . . . here!"

Teina tried to ask another question, but the ghost whizzed away.

A few moments later, the ground started shaking, hanging lights and decorations began swinging, food and other things fell from shelves and tables, crashing sounds could be heard outside, and dust billowed in through the passageway.

Jimox and Teina wrapped their arms and tails around each other, and thought they were going to die.

* * *

Chapter 29: Changes

"We didn't die," Jimox assured the group of Nebador people gathered around the bench listening.

Everyone smiled or chuckled.

Teina grinned. "It was the most humbling experience of our lives, because ..." A fit of coughing took her and she wilted into Jimox' arms.

"Because the Kid's Motorway stations," he continued, "all of them, and several other buildings, had been reduced to piles of rubble, and Teina knew why ..."

*   *   *

Once they overcame their initial shock, the pair moved toward clear air as quickly as they could, coughing as they groped their way deeper and deeper into Fairy Castle. Soon they came to a door labeled *First-Aid Station*, yanked it open, and found a small room with a cot, a chair, and a shelf of supplies. After taking two seconds to memorize the layout, they pulled the door closed behind them, just as the main cloud of dust arrived.

Tails found each other in the darkness and silence.

"Wow ..." Teina began, but couldn't think of anything else to say.

"Let's ... move forward slowly and sit down on the cot," Jimox suggested.

Teina nodded, chuckled, then said, "Okay."

A minute later, after only one banged foot and one bumped head, they managed to get seated.

"What do you think? Ten minutes?" she asked the darkness.

"Let's give it fifteen. That dust was pretty fine."

She nodded, then chuckled again.

*

The dust had mostly settled when they emerged, and the passageway quickly led them to the outside.

"High Alert," Jimox said. "The quake could have damaged the fence."

Teina frowned. "We've been on High Alert for two days!"

"Okay, Double-High Alert."

They looked around. Dust covered everything. The Fairy and Witch's Castles were still standing, but the Knight's Castle, and several smaller buildings, were just piles of rock.

They wandered in silence into Forestland, where a few buildings had collapsed, then around the World Tree, seemingly undamaged, and finally into Machineland, where the Wild Roller Ride was nothing but broken sticks and twisted metal.

When the Machineland Kid's Motorway station came into view, they both stood staring. The quake had completely demolished it.

"And the other motorway stations . . ." Teina began.

"Are built exactly the same way," Jimox finished.

They hurried into Olde Towne, found it mostly in good condition, and quickly arrived at the front of Similand where their home had been reduced to a heap of broken bricks and shattered glass.

Jimox saw the tears on Teina's cheeks, so he wrapped his tail tightly around her.

They poked around the ruins, but couldn't see anything worth saving.

"Do you remember . . ." Teina began, dealing with a lump in her throat, ". . . if our journals were still in there?"

"They were gone, I remember that. I thought of writing a little last night, but couldn't."

She snuffled. "Good. Hopefully they're somewhere in Fairy Castle. I feel done here. Shall we walk the fence?"

Jimox nodded.

The entire city outside of Similand seemed to be silent, still, and covered with dust. No dogs threatened them, although a few wandered aimlessly. The animal-proof fence was a little twisted in places, but still doing its job. When they were about halfway around the theme park, Teina said, "I want to stop at the office building and look at something."

After slipping in through the employee's entrance, Teina led Jimox right to a large map she had seen in a conference room. It depicted all of Similand, and everything built in each decade was shaded a different color.

They perched side-by-side on a table and studied it.

"The Kid's Motorway stations were some of the oldest buildings," Jimox observed.

"And the Knight's Castle."

*   *   *

"We were *very* careful around the old buildings that hadn't collapsed," Jimox explained. "One fell down by itself about a week later. After we hooked up with Nebador, *The Roofers* discovered that another building was unsafe, and knocked it down for us after we pulled out some artworks."

Teina perked up. "Luckily the fence, and the reservoir and water system, were mostly okay, just little problems we could fix."

"The biggest change for us," Jimox went on, "was that we suddenly had a very different relationship with Giona and the ghosts who lingered in Similand . . ."

*   *   *

Chapter 30: Ghosts

Teina stood well-back from the tree and watched the volt meter as Jimox, invisible among the leaves, ran the electric chainsaw. As soon as the saw fell silent, she noted the voltage, but knew he needed a moment to get his ear cups off. "You okay up there?" she finally called.

"Yep, except for all the sawdust in my fur. Undercut's done, and I didn't go too far and get my saw trapped, this time! How's the battery?"

"Eleven point eight, coming back up toward twelve. I think it'll handle the last cut."

"Okay, I'm putting my gear back on."

Soon the saw started buzzing again, and it wasn't long before Teina heard a loud crack and the dead branch tumbled to the ground, breaking into several pieces on impact.

She switched off the inverter.

"I need a shower!" came her partner's voice from the tree. "Saw coming down."

Teina received the chainsaw, dangling from a rope, then a bag containing ear cups, goggles, and saw-adjusting tools. Jimox made his way carefully down through the branches. "Whew!"

"I want a shower too," Teina declared. "I like to be all fresh and pretty when we go out to Ghost Island."

"That's tonight, isn't it?" he asked while coiling the power cord.

"Yeah, and Giona says we have visitors from far away."

"We might hear some new stories!"

Jimox collected the chainsaw and tools, Teina pulled the power wagon, and they headed for the maintenance building behind Olde Towne where they kept it all.

*

As sunset light faded and dusk approached, the pair carried oil lanterns, not yet lit, as they silently stepped into a little boat at the Forestland Lake dock. Their weekly journey to the lake's island, renamed Ghost Island after being set aside as a sanctuary for their non-material friends, was a solemn occasion that made Jimox and Teina want to clean up and dress up a little.

They also knew to be silent most of the time. Many of the lingering spirits who had stories to tell were very shy, after having died untimely or unjust deaths. They had the best chance of sharing if the pair of monkey mammals did little but listen.

Giona was different from most of the other ghosts. Jimox and Teina now knew that she could have moved on to the spirit world long ago, even before they met her, but had chosen to stay behind to help her fellows achieve the same happiness she already enjoyed.

At the little dock on the island, Jimox jumped out and tied up the boat while Teina kept it steady with the oars. Hand in hand they walked up the path toward the clearing. Half-seen misty shapes peeked out from behind trees and bushes, watching and faintly moaning or chattering among themselves.

Fresh, dry rugs and pillows were in place, as always, onto which the pair of guests settled. By agreement, they were no longer in Similand. This island belonged to Giona and the ghosts, to do with as they pleased, without interference from the mortal couple who maintained the rest of the old theme park.

Giona danced into the clearing, the handful of Similand regulars close behind. About a hundred came more slowly, and perhaps a hundred more just watched from the bushes.

"It is an honor to be here, Giona," Jimox announced with an air of formality. "We probably would have died in the quake if you and the other ghosts hadn't . . . um . . . helped us move to Fairy Castle."

Giona giggled and Teina grinned.

The pair fell silent, put arms and tails around each other, and leaned back to see and hear whatever might take place.

✳

As the darkness deepened, more spirits crept out of the trees and shimmered in soft shades of greens and blues, with sometimes a tinge of yellow. The angry reds and oranges that Jimox and Teina remembered from Gibson's Bay and downtown Westron were rarely seen anymore.

With encouragement from Giona, twelve ghosts came forward that evening to tell their stories. What they had to say varied from just a few words, to ten or fifteen minutes of rambling, but in each case the pair of mortals listened carefully. Most of what they heard about Burning Day was the same as they knew from their own hometown in the north. A few stories included injustices that resulted from the fear running wild in the last days of the former civilization. One shy ghost spoke of an abusive parent, and found the courage to rest in Teina's hand when she offered it.

"Weeee!" Giona called in her tiny voice as the abused spirit turned a pure blue and floated up into the sky, never again to be seen or heard on Siminia Three.

✳

Sometime after midnight, Jimox and Teina said good-night to the remaining spirits, less in number by seven or eight. They silently lit their lanterns and made their way back across Forestland Lake.

Jimox rowed, and by the time they came to the far dock, Teina was asleep in the bottom of the boat.

Chapter 31: The Eagles Nest

"*Now* we can tell them about meeting Nebador, *right?*" Teina begged.

Jimox smiled and looked at his listeners. "Except for the plague, and the quake, that was probably the biggest scare of our lives, and it all started at the very top of the World Tree . . ."

* * *

The Castle Kitchen buzzed with activity. The official souvenir album of Fairyland played over speakers hidden in the huge wooden beams. Just outside, through the open doors, the Goblin Fountain trickled and splashed in the golden rays of sunset. Teina dashed in with a bowl of fresh greens.

Jimox, wearing a chef's hat, stirred his macaroni and cheese. "It needs a little garlic powder, I think."

Teina pulled a cutting board close to Jimox, under the one working light bulb. "Yum, I *love* macaroni and cheese! And today I'm using one of our precious jars of marinated artichoke hearts," she said, twisting it open. "How's the battery?" she asked, glancing up at the light.

"This one's pretty good, but we don't have many like it left. We could eat outside . . ."

"Sure. I just need to pick a few bugs out of the salad."

Jimox declared the macaroni ready, shut off the bottled-gas stove, and tossed his hat aside. With trays in hand, they turned off the light and music, and headed out into the warm summer evening.

The Castle Kitchen had tables both inside under the thatched roof, and outside around the Goblin Fountain. Although the two permanent residents of Similand ate somewhere different almost every meal, sometimes outside the theme park, the Castle Kitchen was closest to their dwelling in Fairy Castle.

"It'll be a beautiful, star-studded night!" Teina declared, looking up at the sky. "Wanna sleep in the Eagle's Nest?"

"Yeah! I'll get the binoculars!"

*

They carried flashlights, but the twilight allowed the pair to make the climb without them. Starting at the Olde Towne entrance to the World Tree, ramps, ladders, and balance beams with hand rails took them higher and higher into the great artificial tree. Balance beams without hand rails, and swinging ropes, were both tempting, but they knew the safety nets were rotten, and suspected the ropes might be getting that way.

They passed under roller coaster tracks and over water flumes, the tracks silent for the last twelve years, the flumes dry for just as long.

Eventually they came to the highest point on the World Tree, the Eagle's Nest, the goal of all young climbers from the day the park had opened. Few under eight years of age had ever made it. Even many over eight had discovered a previously-unknown fear of heights at about one hundred and fifty feet, and taken the nearest slide to lower, less frightening, levels.

Teina and Jimox, now eighteen and twenty-two by their reckoning, hardly gave it a thought.

In the Eagle's Nest, tightly-latched ice chests opened and sleeping bags came out. From another, dried fruit emerged. Jimox pulled the binoculars from his day pack, and Teina got out a night-vision scope, less powerful in magnification, but able to gather much more light.

They began with a familiar routine, first scanning their entire beloved Similand for dogs.

"Raccoon over in Machineland," Jimox announced.

"Over by the roller coaster ruins? Yeah, I've seen him. There's that orange cat that works the birds around Forestland Lake."

Satisfied that their precious animal-proof fence was doing its job, they turned their attention to the outside world.

Although it had little practical purpose, this part of their routine was deeply rooted in their childhoods. Without exchanging a word, they peered at the streets and highways, the inter-city rail tracks, the airport several miles away, and the seaport near the horizon. Finding nothing, they exchanged viewing tools and looked again. Both of them sighed.

"Why do we keep doing that?" Teina asked.

Jimox thought for a long moment. "Hope . . . and fear."

Teina chuckled. "Hope that we're not alone. Fear that we're not alone."

Jimox nodded, then lay back on his sleeping bag.

Teina took the night-vision scope again and looked at the tall buildings of downtown Westron, several missing since the quake.

Jimox frowned with thought. "If we saw someone, I'm not sure which emotion I'd feel most. So it's probably best that there's no one."

Teina spoke while continuing to look through the night-vision scope. "Except there's a flying saucer over downtown, shining a light onto the buildings."

✳

They didn't sleep that night.

With the binoculars, they determined it was a sphere, not a saucer. Its bright light seemed to penetrate dirty glass, curtains, maybe even solid walls.

Jimox scanned Similand to make sure they hadn't left any lights on anywhere, and they agreed not to use the flashlights.

They felt fear . . . and hope.

Sometime in the wee hours of the morning, the sphere lowered itself to the ground, very close to the train station, Teina guessed, possibly right in the parking lot.

Still, they couldn't sleep.

They talked about what they would do if the thing moved toward Similand. Thoughts came to them, of hiding in deep, dark basements or tunnels. More thoughts came, of welcoming the aliens, and fixing them macaroni and cheese.

✳

As the sun rose, they munched dried fruit and took turns watching. At least one of them kept an eye on downtown constantly. The other occasionally scanned all other directions.

About mid-morning, the sphere rose from the train station.

It didn't move toward Similand. Instead, it began poking into the mountain canyons north of downtown.

About noon, it disappeared into Oak Canyon, and a few minutes later, a wall of water came gushing out of the canyon, nearly filling the banks of the river that usually held only a trickle.

"I think it zapped Oak Canyon Dam!" Jimox yelled.

Teina took the binoculars, just in time to see the sphere emerge from the canyon and hover over the river. "It's out. It's looking at the river, I think. Whoa!"

"What?"

"It just shot straight up into the sky, almost faster than I could see, like here to the moon in one second flat!"

Jimox searched the sky with his eyes, but found nothing.

✳

For the rest of that day, one of them stayed in the Eagle's Nest, scanning the horizon and the sky, while the other descended to get food and drink, water gardens, or tend solar panels and batteries.

They stayed up there all the next night, taking turns watching downtown, Oak Canyon, and everything else. Their bodies forced them to sleep a little. Their minds still raced.

The next morning, they both realized the danger.

"Oh, no! Our dam in Pine Canyon!"

✳

Jimox and Teina had just worked for five years to turn an abandoned theme park into a beautiful oasis. It was their home, and neither one wanted to give it up.

These thoughts led them to realize that they weren't going to hide. If the ship came back, it was only going to mess with Similand, or Pine Canyon Reservoir, over their dead bodies.

They spent time every day and every night watching the sky. At least once a day, they climbed the World Tree and scanned the horizon from the Eagle's Nest. While they watched, they talked.

After cooling off from their initial reactions, they both admitted that there could have been a good reason for blowing up Oak Canyon Dam. Maybe the quake had damaged it, and it was about to burst. Maybe the aliens thought everyone was dead, and wanted to help the place return to a natural state.

"Well," Teina began. "We'll just have to *tell* them that Pine Canyon Dam is being used, won't we?"

Jimox lowered the binoculars and looked at her.

"What colors of paint do we have?" she continued. "You know, really bright colors."

Jimox grinned with understanding.

＊

While looking over the paint cans in the theme park maintenance buildings, they discussed what to say.

Teina was in favor of trying to figure out the aliens' language. She had seen books on crop circles that attempted to attach meanings to the different shapes that had mysteriously appeared in farmers' fields for centuries.

Jimox pointed out that the books were mostly guessing, and if they did that, they could just as easily be saying, "Please Blow Up This Dam."

Teina sighed.

Eventually they settled on a waterproof bright-red paint used for lines on roads. It would stand out well against the concrete on top of the dam. They also decided to start and end their message with spirals, the most common design from crop circles, but use their own language in between.

With child trailers behind both bicycles, filled with paint cans and brushes, they struggled to pedal even on the level streets. On the slightest slopes, they had to walk. The steep dirt road up to the dam took four trips.

An entire day was consumed by sweeping the top of the dam, but they felt good knowing they were there, ready to shout curses or throw rocks if the ship should approach. They also had guns, but didn't have much hope of winning a real battle against aliens.

Another half day, with measuring tape and chalk, saw their message laid out as neatly as possible in big letters.

Finally, they got busy painting, while still watching the ground for dogs and the sky for alien space ships.

◎ WE'RE USING THIS! DON'T TOUCH! ◎

* * *

Boro laughed heartily. "It's a good thing it's just Nebador out there, and not the big, bad aliens you were imagining!"

Teina's grin was missing several teeth, but her eyes sparkled.

"We hardly slept for a week," Jimox explained, "fearing they would come back, blast the dam to pieces, then come and suck out all our juices."

Mati snickered. "We've seen creatures who would do that, but they're gone now . . . except a few wandering through deep, dark inter-stellar space."

"I'd like to hear *that* story!" Teina said, coughed a few times, then looked at Jimox. "But we should finish ours first."

He kissed her. "Luckily, we only had to wait a week, but when the life-monitor ship Toria Ralora arrived, it just hovered about twenty meters up, right over the Forestland plaza, where landing circle B-One is today."

"Drove us crazy for three days!" Teina managed to say.

"We later found out they had watched us paint the words on the dam from orbit, got a language specialist, figured out what it said, and followed the water pipes with their sensors. Then they just hovered."

"There was a reason . . ." Teina started to say, but couldn't finish.

Jimox waited for her to recover. "But we didn't know what it was until . . . several days later. So the life-monitor ship just waited. At first we watched from hiding places. Then we stood out in the open. Finally we threw a few rocks, but the ship was too high."

Teina grinned and most of the listeners chuckled.

"At last, we were so frustrated that Teina stomped out there, right under the ship, and shouted . . . do you remember what you said?"

She nodded. "You tell them."

"She shouted, *GET YOUR SLIMY GREEN ASSES DOWN HERE SO WE CAN SEE YOU!*"

The entire crew of the Manessa Kwi, the ursine healer, a reptilian assistant host, and about eight others who had gathered around to listen, all howled or shook with laughter.

Jimox and Teina both sat grinning, basking in the memory of one of the most important moments of their lives.

As soon as quiet returned, Jimox finished the story. "Half a minute later, the ship landed, and the ramp nearly scared the pee out of us. A variety of critters emerged, most of whom our animal-proof fence was *supposed* to keep out."

Teina couldn't help but laugh, but soon regretted it.

Jimox held her close. "We were half-expecting to be blasted by ray guns. Instead, all the people from the ship, both crew and specialists, bowed to us."

* * *

Chapter 32: A New Perspective

On the following day, the original station hosts seemed to have more energy than ever before. They came to the Goblin Fountain early and ate breakfast with Brora before anyone else gathered.

Kolarrr'ka, Ashley, and T'sss'lisss arrived next, from the Forestland Hostel, and a few minutes later the crew of the Manessa Kwi staggered into Castleland, yawning and stretching.

Teina, a few breakfast crumbs lingering around her mouth, grinned at them.

Jimox began the day's story. "Okay, so some aliens landed in a flying saucer that was really a flying ball, and it turned out they didn't want to suck out all our juices . . ."

Teina chuckled, then lapsed into coughing.

Everyone waited.

Once Teina was settled, Jimox went on. "We told them it was okay if they blew up every dam on the planet, just not Pine Canyon. They agreed not to touch Pine Canyon. Then we thought they'd go away."

Teina smiled, holding in a funny thought, but managed to avoid the temptation to laugh or talk again.

"They didn't go away," Jimox continued, smiling at Teina.

Teina, still holding in a grin, shook her head to verify.

"They offered us medical exams, told us we were eating too much low-fiber canned food, that we couldn't have children, and a few other things we already knew."

Teina finally cracked a smile.

"And then they dropped a huge bomb on us."

Jimox and Teina both looked around at the expectant faces of their listeners.

"They told us we were the planetary prince and princess of Siminia Three, and that they would do nothing, absolutely nothing, anywhere on our planet, unless it was okay with us."

✳

The station hosts had known this part of the story was coming, but the crew of the Manessa Kwi, and the three young Education Service students, sat with open mouths trying to understand.

"So all those years, bok . . ." Kolarrr'ka began.

Mati frowned. "Being alone after the plague . . ."

"Scrounging for food . . ." Kibi said with a shiver.

"Running from wild dogs . . ." Ilika said, frowning.

"Helping millionsss of ghossstsss . . ." T'sss'lisss remembered, tightening her coils.

Rini squirmed. "Not knowing why you were alive . . ."

"Fixing up Similand . . ." Boro added.

A long moment of silence lingered, so the elderly couple looked at the one guest who hadn't yet spoken.

Ashley swallowed, then whispered one word. "Training."

Teina smiled and nodded.

✳

After everyone had absorbed what the pair had just revealed, Jimox continued. "At first we were afraid they were going to expect us to make big decisions about huge projects right away. You know, which dams to blow up, things like that."

Teina nodded with wide eyes.

"But they knew we needed lots of time to get used to the idea, so they didn't push anything."

Teina swallowed to get ready to speak. "We started *wishing* they would push something."

Jimox nodded. "They stayed in their ship, and wouldn't even *walk around* unless we invited them to!"

Many of the listeners chuckled.

"So we were forced to start thinking, and making some decisions about what *we* wanted out of the situation."

Teina snuggled close to Jimox and buried her face in his white fur. "Children," she mumbled.

Jimox held her close as he explained. "We lived in the very best place on the planet for children — or anyone — to come and play to their hearts' content. But we couldn't have any of our own. It only took us about a week to realize what we wanted to do."

Teina peeked out and nodded, but her eyes were moist and she didn't try to speak.

"We offered to make Similand into a place where anyone in the whole universe who wanted to play or relax could come. We didn't know the proper term for it at the time, but we were offering to create Siminia Three Planet Station, the place where any project, anywhere on the planet or in the solar system, starts and ends with relaxing, re-supplying ships, planning, training sessions, and lots of just plain fun."

At that moment, a reptile zoomed by cranking the pedals of a small, three-wheeled, personal transportation device.

An ursine loped along behind. "I'll meet you at the World Tree!"

Jimox and Teina both grinned with happiness.

* * *

Chapter 33: Plea

The elderly pair retired early that day.

The three Education Service passengers had essays to work on, so they went off to continue their observations and interviews. Four members of Manessa's crew headed for Olde Towne where they were working their way through the museums and attractions. Kibi and Ilika found themselves wandering into Forestland, hand in hand, without a clear plan for the evening.

The sun bathed the planet station in angled shafts of orange-tinted light as it approached the western horizon.

As the captain and steward strolled by Forestland Lake, one of the small rowboats at the dock rocked a little and caught Ilika's eye. "We haven't been out on the lake. Would you enjoy a quiet evening on still water?"

Kibi smiled and wished she could feel romantic, but was worrying too much about the elderly station hosts. "Sure. It will keep my mind off . . . you know."

"I think you're worrying about it more than they are."

"Probably."

Ilika held the little boat while Kibi stepped in, then joined her. They each took an oar and spent the next half hour finding a rhythm that would propel the boat anywhere but in a little circle. They were both laughing so hard they soon forgot all about Jimox and Teina.

*

The waterways of Forestland Lake turned out to be more complex and confusing than the pair of visitors had realized. After they gained some control of the direction and speed of their little vessel, they discovered that fingers of land from both the shore and the three islands made the voyage long, even though the lake was not really that big.

Two of the islands were small, with little docks and two or three picnic tables. One was already occupied, with a rowboat tied up and a crew of reptiles sharing an evening meal. They waved as the pair of monkey mammals passed.

The largest island, Ilika and Kibi knew, was Ghost Island. Signs every eight meters or so along the shore reminded planet station visitors that no mortals were allowed. It appeared to be completely silent and still.

They had passed Ghost Island and were heading back toward the main dock, when suddenly a stiff breeze came out of nowhere, and the inexperienced rowers couldn't make headway. Soon they were exhausted from trying, and decided to give up and wait for the wind to die down.

Kibi happened to look up at the evening sky. Scattered clouds still glowed slightly with sunset light. "Ilika, why are the clouds going in the opposite direction from this wind?"

He shrugged. "Winds often blow in different directions at different altitudes." But even as he said those words, he frowned.

✳

The wind stopped . . . until they tried again to row back to the dock.

Puzzled looks came to both of them when they saw the reptilian crew row across the lake with no difficulty.

Kibi and Ilika remained stuck between two islands, the smallest and the largest. One contained only picnic tables. The other was forbidden.

The captain and his steward conferred and came up with a plan. They would row *around* the small island, which would put them on the same finger of Forestland Lake that the reptiles had just easily crossed.

They put their plan into action, but as soon as they started to gain a little distance from Ghost Island, the wind came up again, blowing them back. This time it didn't let up, and they were forced, against their will, to approach the shore of the forbidden island. Soon they were so close they could read the fine print on one of the signs.

NO MORTALS ALLOWED

except by invitation

Ilika sighed. "I think . . . we're being invited."

Kibi frowned. "More like *kidnapped*."

A gust of wind threatened to shove them right into a thorny bush on the shore of the island.

"Okay, okay!" Ilika barked, and began to row toward the Ghost Island dock.

The wind ceased.

Just as they tied the little boat to the dock, the last light of evening faded from the sky.

✳

In the twilight, Ilika and Kibi held hands as they slowly made their way from the dock to the clearing in the middle of the island.

Kibi began to drag her feet, and Ilika could feel the fear in her tight grip and sweaty hand. He let her set the pace, which slowed to a crawl.

As they inched toward the clearing, Kibi remembered something about rugs and pillows spread out for Jimox and Teina. Only dead leaves and fallen branches greeted the unwilling visitors. Every insect sound and snapping twig made her heart skip a beat, and she gripped Ilika's hand tighter and tighter.

Ilika knew they were being watched.

Kibi knew too, and the feeling made her heart race, her skin tingle, and every hair stand on end.

"They won't . . . hurt us . . . will they?" she mumbled in an unsteady voice.

"There's little they can do to hurt us physically. Affecting the material world is extremely difficult for them. But . . . they have a long history of playing on the emotions of weak people. They don't get far with anyone from Nebador."

Kibi's mind raced, and she realized that many of her Psychic Development lessons had attempted to prepare her for this moment. She just wasn't sure they had succeeded.

"And remember," Ilika went on, "these are NOT the advanced spirits you are used to working with in Nebador. These are more like the wild creatures of your home planet — most of them just want to be left alone, but some are full of pain or hunger."

"I . . . I sense that."

As the darkness deepened, misty shapes began to lurk among the trees, most of them a dull-green color, but often tinged with orange or red.

With wide eyes, Kibi stared into the haunted darkness, and vaguely remembered something about dull-green ghosts in the stories Jimox and Teina had told, but couldn't force her mind to recall the details. And worse than the sickly dull-green, the tinges of angry red and frustrated orange made Kibi shiver.

More by feel than sight, the pair of visitors discovered a fallen log and Ilika coaxed Kibi to sit down.

She hesitated, somehow feeling stronger standing up, until the words of a Nebador teacher came to her. *One of the greatest strengths you can have, especially at trying times, is calmness of spirit.*

They sat down on the log, held each other tightly, and the ghosts came out and began to speak.

*

At first, the ghostly voices were tangled and confused, all trying to speak at once, as if they had not spoken to a mortal in a very long time and were aching to be heard. As the minutes passed and the visitors showed no signs of understanding, but also no desire to run away, the voices slowly became clearer, with only one or two speaking at a time.

"They promised us!" one voice shrieked.

"We tried hard for a hundred years!" another moaned.

A misty dull-green shape swooped through the clearing. "Not fair, not fair, not fair!"

Both Ilika and Kibi started to remember bits of the stories Jimox and Teina had told.

A fuzzy orb, mostly red, jumped out from behind a tree. "They hardly ever visit us anymore!"

"Bad monkey mammals!" a smoky-orange shape declared. "They *deserve* to grow old and die!"

Kibi cringed.

A misty form oozed along the ground like a slug. "They treat us like dirt!"

"Chopped liver!"

"Cow patties!"

Suddenly Kibi bristled, stood up, and planted her hands on her hips while breathing with deep gasps. The clearing fell deathly quiet.

Ilika, still on the log, smiled in the darkness.

"You sound like a bunch of whining brats!" she began. "I *remember* the stories about you. You were the ones responsible for the plague. You were given the opportunity to do community service for a century, and since that time has passed, you must have failed. Am I getting warm?"

The dull-green ghosts lost their tinges of color and slunk behind trees or under dead leaves.

"Very warm," Jimox' voice said from the darkness.

Teina activated her bracelet light to reveal both elderly hosts, one on each side of Brora the healer. Behind came Rrr'tana the station host.

Kibi wasn't finished. With a little light in the clearing, she took several steps forward and continued speaking. "When I was eight years old, I was forced to become a slave for the rest of my youth. All you whiners had easy childhoods, got good educations, then wormed your way into positions of power in your biological weapons labs. That's why you were judged, by the planetary prince and princess, many years ago, to be guilty of creating the disease that destroyed your civilization!"

While catching her breath, Kibi glimpsed Teina nodding.

"And I can see why you failed your community service," Kibi went on. "You're still whining, to this day, instead of finding something you can do to contribute to the universe!"

Kibi, feeling completely exhausted, stumbled backwards and plopped down on the log beside Ilika, who quickly put an arm around her.

A large, glowing purple orb formed high in the trees over the clearing and slowly descended.

"Arantiloria," Kibi, looking up, whispered.

Ilika, also recognizing their training specialist, nodded.

Jimox and Teina glanced up, then continued moving forward into the clearing.

The dull-green ghosts tried to find holes to slink into, but some greater power kept them from hiding or running away.

Jimox reached inside himself for strength he hadn't used in many years. "How *dare* you force our guests onto this island against their will!" he boomed.

"Never again!" Teina sputtered, but could find no more breath.

"You are pathetic little ghosts with small minds," Jimox continued. "You led empty lives, giving nothing to the world while you grabbed all the money and power you could find. You chose not to think about what you were creating in your laboratory."

Teina swallowed several times and found her voice. "Giona, the most noble and powerful ghost of all, who is now in advanced classes at the local universe capital, was once a *waitress* in a small town."

Jimox nodded. "You will get the remainder of your thousand years of community service, but not here, and not at any of our retreats. Go!"

Arantiloria became a small purple ball and descended onto the log beside Ilika. The dull-green ghosts, with only about eight hundred and sixty years, by their reckoning, in which to find something worthwhile to do with themselves, dashed away in all directions, never again to be seen or heard at Siminia Three Planet Station.

✳   ✳   ✳

Chapter 34: Kibi's Ghosts

Kibi lay awake for hours going over and over in her mind the events on Ghost Island. When she finally fell asleep beside Ilika, she dreamed.

Big machines on wheels clanged and chugged as they went to and fro in a dark, ugly building, pulling levers and turning valves. Soon things started exploding, and the clanging machines ran out all the exit doors to save themselves. Just an instant before the entire building burst into flames, a hundred or more tiny voices cried out from rows of little cages.

Kibi flew out of her dream, tried to stand, and fell onto the floor.

Ilika was quickly beside her, calling for soft lighting as he tried to determine if she was hurt.

Kibi soon figured out where she was, then collected her wits and relaxed. "Very strange dream . . ."

Ilika helped her back onto the bed.

Suddenly she looked at him with wide eyes. "We missed something last night. We have to go back to Ghost Island!"

"Is tomorrow . . ."

"No, now! Tomorrow could be too late."

✳

Ilika wasn't completely sure Kibi knew what she was doing, until they arrived at the Forestland Lake dock, in the dark hour before first light of dawn, to find Jimox, Teina, and Brora getting into a boat by bracelet light.

Teina looked at Kibi. "Did you have a dream, too?"

Kibi nodded.

"That means we'll need you."

Ilika's doubts disappeared as he got another rowboat ready.

✳

The four monkey mammals and one ursine crept onto Ghost Island silently, save for Teina's occasional cough. They settled onto old logs or the leaf-covered ground in the only clearing on the island.

Kibi fully intended to just watch and learn, following Jimox and Teina's lead in everything that happened.

Ilika felt his only role was to support Kibi.

The two old planet station hosts sat calmly and silently, so Kibi and Ilika did the same.

A quarter hour passed with no sign of anything stirring, except an insect or two.

After half an hour, Brora shifted positions.

Three-quarters of an hour into the vigil, all four monkey mammals stretched their legs but otherwise remained silent.

A few minutes later, all at about the same moment, Ilika shivered, Kibi felt a tingling in her bones, and Teina cocked her head, listening intently.

After a long minute, they all relaxed, as whatever had caused the sensations was gone.

"Kibi," Jimox whispered, "please set your bracelet to pick up audio frequencies outside the audible range, shift into the audible, and amplify."

Kibi worked with her bracelet for a moment, then cringed as five thumping noises, each at a slightly different speed, drowned out all other sounds.

"Our heartbeats," Ilika said. "Sub-sonic."

Kibi instructed the little device to filter them out.

A constant scratching sound began that Brora identified as insect wings, normally ultra-sonic. Kibi eliminated them from the amplified sounds.

Finally, her bracelet fell silent, except for occasional sounds they could identify as coming from themselves or the forest creatures around them. They sat silently and waited.

✳

Kibi had lost track of time when a tiny scream came from her bracelet, then they heard a scurrying sound that quickly faded away. It caused both Teina and Jimox to jerk their heads toward the far side of the island where no trail penetrated and no boat dock was available.

After she was sure the event had passed, Teina spoke in a whisper. "That didn't sound like a monkey mammal to me. In my dream, it was caged lab animals screaming."

"Mine, too," Kibi whispered.

"And that scurrying sound *wasn't* coming from Kibi's bracelet," Jimox declared. "Let's see if it repeats," he suggested.

"You think it's a residual haunting?" Teina asked softly.

"That's my hunch."

✳

About a quarter hour later, a hint of dawn light was creeping into the sky when the scream came again, and the same scurrying sound, seemingly going in the same direction as before.

"You were right," Teina admitted. "But there was no biological weapons lab in Similand!"

"But what if . . ." Jimox began, pondering the evidence as he spoke, ". . . what if the guilty ghosts we chased away yesterday were still practicing some of their old bad habits . . ."

Teina's eyes snapped open wide. "Keeping some weak little animal ghosts captive? I'm going to wring their . . ." A coughing fit took her and she couldn't finish her sentence, but everyone got the meaning.

In the growing dawn light, as the group picked their way through the trees toward the part of Ghost Island where no mortal had set foot in more than two centuries, Jimox spoke. "A residual haunting is an important event that gets recorded by the spirits of a place, and is played back under certain conditions, such as when a visitor is receptive to those events. Didn't you say you were a slave once, Kibi?"

"Yes," she confirmed while climbing over a fallen log.

Teina nodded with understanding as she paused to catch her breath before even attempting the log. "But I think . . . this is much more . . . recent . . ." A deep coughing fit took her and she wilted into Brora's strong arms.

"I don't think Teina is up to this journey," the healer asserted, looking at Ilika and Kibi.

Teina looked frustrated, but eventually nodded and spoke in a whisper. "They called *you*, Kibi. I'm sure you can do whatever needs to be done."

Kibi wasn't as sure as Teina, but she remained silent as the healer and her two charges make their way back to the Ghost Island boat dock, one of them coughing almost constantly.

Not far beyond the log, Kibi and Ilika came upon a tiny clearing formed by three trees growing close together. Kibi again felt the tingling in her bones as they stopped and stared at the ground.

Ilika couldn't suppress a shiver.

In the clear area under the trees, twigs had been carefully poked into the soil and woven with other twigs to form a little symbolic fence around a space less than a meter across.

A dozen or more animal screams suddenly came from Kibi's bracelet. Ilika recognized the cries of small mammals, the squawks of frightened birds, and the hisses of cornered reptiles before Kibi cancelled the amplification.

In the minute of silence that followed, Ilika could see Kibi collecting herself and thinking about what to do.

"I don't know enough about what's going on here, Ilika. I wish Teina and Jimox could have stayed."

"We are here because they need to pass on many of their responsibilities. I can't think of a better person for this task than a highly-intuitive steward who has a deep love and respect for animals."

Kibi tried to smile, but her smile quickly faded. "Let's . . . sit down on the ground just outside the little fence."

The ground was soft and free of weeds and stickers under the three trees. Each of them found a small space between two trees, leaving one side of the triangle of trees open, the side to the east, closest to the edge of the planet station and the wilderness beyond.

After another minute of thoughtful silence, Kibi spoke. "At first I was wondering why they didn't just leave. These twigs couldn't keep in a *living* animal, much less a ghost. But before I even finished thinking the question, I knew the answer."

Ilika looked at her.

"Fear," she said, "and who better to understand fear than a slave."

Ilika nodded. "Don't forget that frightened animals sometimes bite and scratch."

"Yeah, I know. Just the price of . . . being a steward."

She tapped her bracelet to resume the frequency shift and amplification that would allow them to hear the little ghost voices again. Even as the tiny screams, squawks, and hisses returned, Kibi began humming a simple tune, almost a lullaby, and carefully, twig by twig, taking down the symbolic fence.

*

Boro and Sata sat on the Forestland Lake dock as Ilika and Kibi rowed across the lake in the morning light.

"Brora said we'd find you guys here," Sata called.

As the captain and steward got close, scratches on their faces and hands could be easily seen.

"What happened to *you* two?" Boro asked as he received the rope from Kibi and tied it to the dock.

Kibi grinned. "Oh . . . just some twigs where they shouldn't have been."

Ilika laughed.

Sata narrowed her eyes with suspicion, but knew Kibi wouldn't tell the story until she was good and ready.

* * *

Chapter 35: Badly-Needed Help

Later that morning, the elderly couple arrived at the Goblin Fountain smiling and ready to begin the next chapter of their story, as if the hard part was behind them and the rest would be easy.

Kibi wondered if it had something to do with recent events on Ghost Island.

"The next eight years of our lives were more fun than any monkey mammal deserves to have," Jimox began with a gleam in his eyes.

Teina nodded. "We started with landing circles — we didn't want space ships parking just anywhere, dripping space-oil or whatever." She grinned at her audience and they howled or honked with laughter, Boro most of all.

Seeing that Teina was almost blue from speaking, Jimox took over. "And every time we started something, a ship would appear with just the right tools, supplies, helpers, and knowledge. With the landing circles, it was reptiles with surveying equipment, and they knew just how big the circles should be."

Teina snickered. "We actually did one before they got here, and it looked like a lumpy frog!"

Kolarrr'ka clucked and Mati grinned.

Jimox smiled. "Since Forestland had the biggest landing circle, big enough for a life-monitor ship, we made the nearby snack bar into a supply depot, and we changed a little storeroom into an office."

Teina grinned at the memory.

"And less than an hour after we decided to do that, and were just sweeping up leaves and talking about it, ships landed and supply cabinets came floating out!"

Rini chuckled. "That confused us about Nebador for a while, but now we understand."

Teina smiled at the freckled lad. "Then *The Roofers* came!" she announced.

"That's why the buildings are more than two centuries old, and still good, except the ones we lost in the quake."

"And when they saw us picking through fourteen-year-old canned food . . ." Teina began, but had to stop and rest.

Jimox made sure his partner was okay before continuing. "They showed up with cabinets full of food, and gardeners lined up with rakes and shovels, ready to work in our gardens, which were just little weed patches then, with a few edible weeds."

Teina laughed, but regretted it and nearly turned blue.

"And they've kept all the nutrition cabinets stocked ever since," Jimox soon went on, "with plenty of foods we like, and stuff for everyone in the Nebador Services. But we still went scrounging and picking through what was left from our civilization, just because a can of tekle fruit, or sweet goma beans, when we found a good one, would bring back memories from our childhoods like nothing else could."

Teina swallowed. "But the day came when we couldn't find any more good ones."

"About a hundred years ago," Jimox explained with a note of sadness.

✳

After a break for snacks and medicine, the couple was eager to continue.

Jimox began. "We snuck into the big restaurant in Olde Towne, to make it into a museum, when no one was watching so we could work alone."

Arantiloria, currently in her purple-haired human form, laughed deeply.

The furry monkey mammals both grinned.

"We barely got it ready . . ." Teina began, then swallowed and looked at Jimox.

". . . before the first ship landed, right outside the front door, with art works from all over the planet for us to sort out."

The entire audience chuckled or clucked.

"They apologized . . ." Teina said.

". . . for doing it without asking us," Jimox explained, "but it was all stuff that was in danger of being ruined by leaky roofs — mostly paintings and books."

"We weren't angry," Teina said.

"How could we be? There they were, paintings so famous we remembered seeing pictures of them when we were children. A few were already damaged. The specialists on the ship explained that Westron had the best climate for keeping the rest in good shape — warm and dry."

"They wanted us to go with them to museums and galleries . . ." Teina began, but had to stop and catch her breath.

". . . and sometimes we did," Jimox picked up the story, "especially to places like our home town in the north. But working through huge museums full of musty old paintings in far-away lands can get *pretty* boring for young monkey mammals!"

Most of the audience nodded with understanding.

"Next we cleaned out souvenir shops for meeting rooms . . ." Teina shared.

"Hauled in stacks of mattresses from hotels around here to make hostels . . ." Jimox added.

"And turned a quiet corner of Forestland into a meditation area," Teina said, then had to stop and concentrate on breathing for a minute.

"But the fun part," Jimox said as he rubbed his partner's back, "was all the toys and adventures!"

Teina sparkled. "Wagons, bicycles, tricycles, pedal cars . . ."

"Beach balls, plastic bowling pins, and a thousand other outdoor toys!"

"Little row boats and canoes . . ."

"Similand never had any of that stuff," Jimox explained. "It was mostly high-tech so people would pay money to get in."

"Nebador didn't need high-tech," Teina continued the thought. "Nebador people needed a *break* from flying starships and working on star stations!"

The six Transport Service crew members all nodded vigorously.

"But the very most fun . . ."

Teina grinned, guessing what Jimox was about to say.

"You want to share it?" he asked, looking at her.

She shook her head.

"The most fun for us — and it took us about twenty years to get them all done — was creeping through the old rides and figuring out how to make them into real, live adventures, even though most of them didn't work anymore."

"Nebador technicians restored a couple that had some historical importance," Teina managed to say.

Mati nodded.

"And a few," Jimox continued, "work about like they used to . . ."

Boro grinned.

". . . but many of them are *very* different now, much more challenging and — if you're not prepared — *dangerous*."

Ashley smiled and nodded knowingly.

✳

The old couple took a nap, but were back as soon as they awoke.

Brora didn't look pleased.

"All the crews and specialists, who came to help in any way, knew we had to learn the language of Nebador," Jimox began, "so each one gave us a new word or two. After a few years, we were speaking it, and didn't even notice when the ones who spoke *our* language weren't there. It's amazing how different a word can sound from mammal to avian to insect."

"We *know*," Ashley muttered, rolling her eyes.

Teina grinned at the young furless monkey mammal. "Tell them about the music!" she begged, turning to Jimox.

"Oh, yeah. Our collection of good deep-cycle batteries was down to almost nothing, and it was hard to keep even a little music box going while we worked. But of course someone noticed, and a ship showed up with little matter-energy converters.”

Teina smiled. “We loved to dance back then, nothing fancy, just moving our feet and tails to a good beat.”

“So it didn’t take us long to rig up background music and sound effects in about a dozen places, and a big music box at the dance floor in each land, with a huge collection of music to choose from.”

“And?” Teina coaxed.

“Oh, and we put tumbling mats on each dance floor so everyone could use them without hurting themselves.”

“And?” Teina prodded urgently.

“Oh yeah, and video players in four different theaters so Nebador people could watch our old movies.”

Teina stuck out her tongue at Jimox, then turned to the listeners. “And so *we* could watch them for the first time in about twenty years!”

✳

After several visitors compared favorite movies with the elderly hosts, Jimox got a far-away look in his eyes.

“What?” Teina asked, looking at him.

“I was just remembering Kasssor-k’m.”

Teina nodded. “We need to go visit him, even though he *says* he prefers to be alone.”

After a long moment of silence had passed, the couple remembered their audience. “By the time we got those matter-energy converters, Siminia Three Planet Station was a very busy place,” Jimox explained.

“Yeah!” Teina verified. “Eight, sometimes twenty ships a day!”

“We loved seeing all those scientists, navigators, educators — the cream of the cream of the universe — all coming here to ride tricycles and throw beach balls . . .”

The audience chuckled.

“. . . but even though we had lots of help with little things, we were still the *Station Hosts On Duty*, all day, all night, every day, and we were about to DIE of exhaustion!”

“It was our own fault,” Teina muttered.

Jimox nodded. “It was our baby, and we just never thought we’d want any help . . .”

“Until we started *falling down* when we were supposed to be directing a ship to a landing circle,” Teina said softly.

Several listeners moaned with sympathy.

“But Nebador did the right thing,” Jimox went on. “They waited for *us* to ask for help. I mean, we *were* the planetary prince and princess!”

Teina grinned at her partner.

“So this technician — a lizard setting up music and video players — asked where we wanted the extra matter-energy converters and other spare stuff, so we picked out a little storeroom in Olde Towne . . .”

"Then he asked if ..." Teina tried to say, but had to stop and cough deeply.

"He asked if we'd like some monitors so we could see anywhere in the station, and the whole animal-proof fence."

Teina nodded while coughing, and managed to sputter out, "We danced with joy!"

"That storeroom was our first control room," Jimox said, "but we soon moved it to the tower in Fairy Castle."

"And the lizard stayed ..."

"And became our dearest friend. We loved the control room, with windows that looked out in every direction, but didn't want to sit there all the time — we wanted to be out talking to people, stocking the nutrition cabinets, and checking the music players. We asked him to be an assistant host about a year later. He always did everything just the way we taught him, and we soon trusted him with *everything!*"

✳ ✳ ✳

Chapter 36: First Transport

"Sometimes," Jimox began on a cloudy but warm morning, "two ships, at different ends of the station, needed us at once. It happened most often when a passenger transport came in."

Teina's eyes grew large. "Oh, yeah, passenger transports. That's a story they *have* to hear!"

✳ ✳ ✳

"Siminia Three Planet Station, this is passenger transport Triluli Paloma," a reptilian voice began from Teina's bracelet, "one hundred kilometers west at four thousand meters, requesting landing instructions."

She looked at Jimox with wide eyes. "We've never had a passenger transport. How big are they?"

He shrugged.

She touched her bracelet. "Triluli Paloma, how big a landing space do you need?"

"It's supposed to be a hundred and twenty meters across, but the pilot swears she can squeeze us into a hundred."

Jimox and Teina looked at each other.

"B-One is thirty-six meters across," Teina began, "and that's our biggest."

Jimox nodded. "The Castleland Plaza is about fifty. Remember, we decided not to put a landing circle there because of all the trees."

Teina nodded. "That leaves . . . the ticket plaza."

"But it's outside the . . ."

"I know. You get guns, I'll get marker cones."

Jimox strode toward the office in Forestland as Teina touched her bracelet and headed toward the front of the theme park. "Triluli Paloma, this could be an adventure in itself . . ."

*

The passenger transport ship hovered a hundred meters above the large open space just outside the planet station. The pilot and navigator carefully analyzed every bench, planter, drinking fountain, and ticket booth, and discovered they had a circle of clear space a hundred and seven meters across.

The avian crew of the only other ship in the station, having heard the transmissions, gathered near the two hosts at the animal-proof fence. The huge passenger transport extended struts and lowered itself to the ground. A long ramp appeared, but the hatch remained tightly closed.

Jimox checked each pistol and handed a belt with two holsters to Teina. Some of the avians looked nervous, but the feathered engineer offered to work the gate, and the captain and steward spread wings and flapped up to the top of the fence.

Once both hosts were ready, Teina touched her bracelet. "As soon as we're in position, your people must head straight into the planet station, not stopping for anything, no matter what they see or hear."

The reptilian navigator acknowledged that everyone was ready.

Jimox nodded to the bird at the gate, he and Teina slipped out, and the gate quickly closed behind them.

*

During the next minute, with Jimox on watch, Teina marked off a corridor with bright green cones. They met halfway between the ship and the gate.

Jimox pointed. "There's a brown mutt nosing around behind the old stroller rental place, but I can't tell if it's alone. I'll take this side."

Teina got into position to cover the opposite side, then touched her bracelet. "We're ready."

The hatch opened, and the passengers came pouring down the ramp. The planet station hosts didn't dare look, but both cringed when they heard the voices of several young children.

Everything went smoothly, and about a hundred of the passengers were safely inside the animal-proof fence, when Teina was forced to fire the first shot as a trio of large black dogs came running into the ticket plaza.

The crew of the transport ship, and their passengers, had been ready for anything — except the deafening sound of the pistols. The adults mastered their surprise, but one young ursine panicked and ran.

Teina got all three black dogs, but one tumbled into the passenger corridor before dying, causing more panic. A leggy young equine bolted, came face to face with a hungry dog just a second before Jimox shot it, and dashed back to the safety of the corridor and the fence.

Suddenly Teina had a big problem. The young ursine was in her field of fire, and two scuzzy gray dogs were crouching to attack. She took aim at one dog, but the sound of wing-beats filled the air, so she waited, saw the avian captain scoop up the little bear, then shot both dogs with two bullets.

Her field of fire clear, she turned to check on Jimox, and found he also had a clear field. The ship's hatch was closed, and the last few passengers were hurrying through the gate. The pair of monkey mammals walked backwards, side by side, guns still drawn, and were the last ones in before the avian engineer closed the gate.

A moment later, the captain swooped down, back-winged with powerful strokes, and deposited the ursine child on the ground.

"Wow!" the little bear said. "This place is fun!"

* * *

Chapter 37: The Wilderness Outside

After the elderly hosts ran out of steam, about mid-afternoon, Sata decided the time was right for another adventure, a very personal adventure that she had been putting off. She made excuses why she couldn't join both Boro and Kibi for things they wanted to do, then wandered by the Manessa Kwi to get a sun hat and a couple of nutrition bars. She wasn't sure exactly how long her adventure would take.

When she arrived at the old front entrance to the theme park, she found Ilika sitting on a low stone wall gazing across the ancient ticket plaza. Beyond that, weeds, bushes, and small trees were slowly reclaiming the paved parking lot.

"You curious about the world outside the fence too?" she asked, hopping onto the wall beside him.

"Yeah. That story about the first passenger transport got me and Kibi thinking, and we're planning to go out tomorrow if we can. It was one of the largest cities on the planet. Research teams often study the decay process, but this is the first time I've taken a good look at it."

"At first, the stories about wild dogs everywhere had me a little scared," Sata admitted.

"That would have been a dangerous time to live through," Ilika said, "but now all the wild creatures are back in balance, and a dry climate like this can't support very many large carnivores — about one every eight square kilometers, Rrr'tana tells me."

Sata nodded. "I have about four hours of daylight," she said, glancing at the sun as she adjusted her sun hat.

"You sure you want to go alone?"

Sata was silent for a few seconds, but then spoke firmly. "Yeah."

*

The first few times Sata startled a bird or a rabbit-like creature, she nearly ran back to the safety of the planet station and its animal-proof fence.

But this adventure, this step in her on-going process of getting comfortable with the universe, had very little to do with the creatures of the wilderness that could scare her. She had traveled around her home kingdom with her fellow crew members, and knew all about animals who were more afraid of her than she was of them.

True, the creatures on Siminia Three were a little different than those on her home planet, but also very much the same in the ways they lived their lives.

No, this adventure was all about Sata of Sonmatia Three being alone, without Ilika or Boro near, and without a ship, star station, or animal-proof fence to protect her.

After her heart quit racing from the bird who suddenly took flight almost right in her face, Sata breathed slowly and glanced at her mission bracelet. *I could have left you behind, too,* she thought. *But Ilika would have yelled at me.   Besides, what monkey mammal, anywhere, would go into the wilderness without at least a big knife. You're my big knife, little bracelet. But I hope I don't have to use you. I hope I can do this all by myself.*

Any paving that had been thin, or made of small tiles or blocks, was now completely broken up by bushes and trees, and its original surface unrecognizable. Occasionally a street or walkway had been built of large, thick blocks, and these provided paths through the scrubby woods, even though tree roots had begun to tilt some of the blocks.

Sata peered up at a multi-story hotel to her left. Most of the glass was now broken, leaving the concrete rooms and their moldy furniture open to the wind and rain. Plants had established themselves on the bottom two or three floors, and Sata spotted a cat-like creature climbing a woody vine from one room to another.

Above the third floor began the domain of birds, and Sata could faintly hear their cooing and clucking. As she watched, a large raptor spread its wings and took flight from one of the highest rooms.

After taking several deep breaths, she trudged on through the bushes.

The piles of weedy rubble, on both sides of her, had once been houses, Sata finally decided. Occasionally a bit of tile roof was still visible, but only because it was the last thing to fall onto the heap.

A growling sound, coming from somewhere under the rubble, made her freeze. She waited, straining to see or hear where it was coming from, a finger poised over her mission bracelet, her feet ready to run.

Then another sound made her re-think the situation. The whimpering of several puppies was making the mother dog growl louder, but still not show herself.

Sata felt her heart return to a more normal rhythm. "They're not very smart at that age, are they?" she asked the unseen creature, a mammal like herself, and another female.

The growling continued, but without such a desperate tone.

"You have nothing to fear from me, little mommy. I'm from Nebador."

The low warning growl continued. Sata took another deep breath and walked on.

✳

The large grocery store had once boasted a high ceiling and aisle after aisle of food from every corner of Siminia Three. Now only rusting steel columns pierced the rubble, a mixture of ancient roofing materials, rusted cans, and broken jars.

From a low mound, Sata surveyed the ruins, still hosting few bushes and trees because of the thick concrete floor. She could imagine Jimox and Teina, in their youth, selecting their favorite foods to take back to Similand, talking and laughing as they worked.

It occurred to Sata that free food, while it lasted, and free admission to Similand, were the only payments their people gave them for the task of witnessing and recording the end of a civilization, the only payments their people *could* give them.

Sata blinked away the moisture that had gathered in her eyes when she suddenly heard a digging sound, and quickly looked for its source. Not far away, a rabbit-like creature had not noticed the visitor, and was burrowing into the rubble.

Before she could even think, something furry leapt from a nearby bush. The rabbit squeaked once, then fell silent, its neck held tightly from behind in the powerful jaws of a large cat.

Sata didn't dare move, but her heart raced and her mind reviewed the bracelet code she would use if the cat took an interest in *her*.

Minutes that seemed like hours passed slowly as the cat held its prey in a death-grip. Finally the cat began dragging its meal, now completely limp, toward a dense bush.

Sata let out her breath, but then realized she had done so too loudly. The cat dropped its kill, glared at her with two bright eyes, and hissed, but didn't abandon the fresh kill.

For a moment, Sata felt fear. Words from her native language came to her, judgmental words to label the cat as evil for killing the helpless little rabbit.

Sata kept breathing, and began to remember who and what she now was — the navigator of a deep-space response ship, and in training for all other positions on her ship. She was also the survivor of a Great Transformation, had completed fourteen classes on Satamia Star Station, and had begun the Psychic Development program.

From Basic Ecology she knew that a planetary biosphere was a complex web of constantly-flowing streams of energy, and some of those consisted of carnivores catching, killing, and eating their prey. If they didn't, Sata remembered, the biosphere would become imbalanced, the herbivores would grow too numerous, exhaust their food supplies, and soon die of starvation and disease.

She took a slow, deep breath. "I understand. It's yours, and I won't try to take it away from you."

The cat hissed again.

Without taking her eyes off the carnivore, Sata backed away from the ancient grocery store.

✳

More mounds that had once been houses came and went, another multi-story concrete building, and two more stores, all just ruins.

Sata was beginning to feel more confidence in herself as she wandered through this strange mixture of dead civilization and living ecosystem.

The path with fewest bushes suddenly angled downhill. She looked out over the low area and saw that the bushes and trees were greener not far ahead. Her curiosity piqued, she followed the path down.

The stream was barely a trickle, but marks on the trees and rocks showed that water a meter deep sometimes flowed. A bush full of birds exploded with fluttering wings when Sata came into sight, and a wiry dog looked up from getting a drink at the stream, then vanished into the bushes.

From the boulder where Sata nibbled a nutrition bar, she glimpsed two rabbits, and not much later a snake that could have been a tiny version of T'sss'lisss. Soon a large bird arrived who was intent on having snake for dinner, but because of the thick branches, had to make a new plan.

As the sun neared the horizon, and Sata judged she had another hour of daylight, she said good-bye to the little stream and its community of wild creatures.

✳

Not long after she returned to higher ground, Sata's heart began to beat faster as she discovered that all the ruins and faint pathways looked the same, and none of them felt familiar. She took some deep breaths and forced herself to think.

"The sun's at a lower angle," she muttered to herself. "And I'm looking at everything from the opposite direction."

She walked on, but soon came to a halt, as the scrubby trees and mounds were starting to appear completely wrong. She felt herself trembling slightly.

"You're a *navigator!* You're not *supposed* to get lost!"

A lizard raised its head when it heard the frustrated monkey-mammal voice, then quickly backed away into its bush.

With her heart now pounding loudly in her chest, Sata struggled to think of a plan. She looked at her mission bracelet, and could think of three or four ways it could easily save her.

But she didn't *want* it to save her. She was a navigator, and she should be able to get home from a short walk in the wilds.

With panic threatening to rise inside her, she turned one complete circle and spotted the answer. Just a few hundred meters to her right, a six or seven-story concrete building jutted from the trees and bushes. All the windows were broken, and birds came and went constantly. From the roof, or one of the upper floors, she'd be able to see Siminia Three Planet Station and plan her route.

With a sigh and a shiver, Sata suddenly felt renewed hope that her little walk wouldn't end in embarrassing disaster after all.

*

Behind a tangled clump of bushes, Sata found a rusting stairway door kept closed with a rock, and wondered if Teina and Jimox had once prowled through this same building. The ancient hinges creaked and jerked as she pulled, as if fighting to keep her out.

The concrete stairs felt crumbly under her feet. In the dim light filtering down from small broken windows, she saw cracks in the steps, and the rusting metal bars that still held the building together. Sata remembered the original hosts telling about the quake that had shaken the area, bringing down many old brick buildings. As she slowly climbed, dry leaves, twigs, and a few small bones made the stairs tricky. She continued taking slow, careful steps upward.

After a quarter hour of climbing, the door to the roof was locked, but so rusty it crumbled to pieces when Sata pulled. She snorted and spat as the red dust settled, then stepped through.

Weeds and stickers covered the flat roof, but appeared all dry and dead. Sata could imagine it quickly coming to life after a rain, then returning to its dry, dormant state. With her back to the setting sun, she worked her way across the roof, hoping the planet station would be visible from the eastern side.

Sata smiled for the first time in an hour. Siminia Three Planet Station was right about where it should be, but she could have easily missed it if she had just wandered aimlessly through the bushes.

She felt like a navigator again, and remembered several times when the Manessa Kwi had been piloted to higher altitudes for a better view.

As she scanned the landscape and noted the relative positions of several other tall buildings, the sun found the horizon behind her.

Sata swallowed, and a moment later her mission bracelet chimed.

*

"I'm glad you're okay," Kibi's voice reassured.

"I wouldn't be much of a navigator if I got lost, now would I?" Sata teased.

Kibi chuckled. "I got lost in Olde Towne today! Had to ask directions at a response ship of equines."

Sata laughed to release her nervousness. "I know where I am, but I'm just a little too far to do it in the dark."

"Want Manessa to come get you?"

Sata was silent for a moment. "No. I want to finish exploring this old building, and I've got a nutrition bar, so I'll stay here and come back in the morning. All I have to do is talk the local birds into sharing one of their rooms."

Sata couldn't see Kibi's grin of understanding. "Okay! Call if you need anything!"

"See you tomorrow!"

*

After descending to the top floor, Sata quickly discovered that it was a hotel, and all the rooms were completely filthy with bird droppings, nests, and moldy shredded furniture.

"Not Nebador birds," she mumbled to herself.

Although the hallway was clear, it smelled of mold from the leaking roof above, and she hardly dared breath the air. Yanking open a few unmarked doors, she discovered that the closets of bedding and towels were filled with mushrooms and slime.

Returning to the stairwell, Sata had an idea. She remembered that the bottom two or three floors had been completely invaded by plants and small animals. She now knew that the roof was leaking, making the top floor, and maybe others, very unpleasant. Birds owned all the guest rooms when other animals couldn't get to them. She wondered if anything remained in between, so she activated her bracelet light and began to carefully descend the stairs.

*

The fifth floor was damp and moldy, but the fourth made Sata smile. She chuckled when she saw two-hundred-year-old cookies in the rusty vending machine, and thought of Jimox and Teina, but left the cookies alone. The broom and mop closet boasted no comforts, but the bedding closet was just what she had in mind.

After checking the rest of the hallway on that floor to make sure nothing could creep in and surprise her, Sata made herself a nest from ancient blankets, tore open her last nutrition bar, and breathed a deep sigh of satisfaction.

* * *

Chapter 38: A Recurring Dream

As full darkness descended over Siminia Three Planet Station, Brora scanned her two charges for any warning signs, then measured out the medicine that would allow each to sleep easier. They didn't see the slight frown that crossed her face.

Once the planetary prince and princess were curled up together in their favorite room in Fairy Castle, the ursine healer went out to check on the two injuries she knew of among the ships in the station, and whoever else might have banged themselves up that day in adventures and play.

* * *

Six-year-old Teina started crying.

Her mother kept turning on all the stove burners, and putting things directly on top of them — bags of flour, plastic containers of left-overs, and anything else handy.

The smoke and stench was terrible. Twice Teina crept into the kitchen while her mother wasn't looking and turned off the burners, but couldn't do anything about the smoldering food.

The second time, her mother wandered into the kitchen, talking to herself and gazing around like she was lost. She snapped out of it just long enough to spank her daughter hard. "I'm *trying* to cook dinner!" Then she turned the burners back on and resumed her aimless mumbling.

Tears streaming down her face, Teina ran toward the back door.

Her father was in the carport, washing the car with the engine running, using a rag and generous splashes from a gasoline can.

"Stop it, Daddy!"

He glared at his daughter with crazed eyes. "*You* want to do it?" he asked with a demented tone, offering her the rag and gasoline can.

Teina ran to her room, grabbed a beloved doll, and sat on her bed.

Suddenly an explosion tore away half the house.

Teina cried for a minute, then abruptly stopped and looked around. Smoke was creeping under her door, colored red-orange from flames in the hallway beyond. The only window led to the front of the house.

Teina wasn't supposed to open her window. The air conditioning wouldn't work with it open.

The six-year-old girl looked at the smoke one more time. Her eyes narrowed, and she scanned the room with a new purpose. Her wooden toy box was the heaviest thing she could lift, just a little, if she tried very hard.

Straining with all her might, she got it up to her bed, put her doll inside, and picked up the box again.

As smoke started swirling around her, Teina ran toward the window as fast as her legs would go.

The shock and sound of breaking glass swirled all around her until everything, an eternity or perhaps just a second later, came to rest on the front lawn.

She saw her doll in front of her, picked it up, and ran. She didn't feel the cuts on her arms and legs until much later. She didn't pay attention to the other houses that were burning. She just ran, as fast as she could go, toward her favorite patch of woods, two blocks away.

And she didn't cry again for almost a year.

* * *

Jimox was awakened by his precious partner thrashing and whimpering in pain and confusion. He wrapped his arms around her. "Bad dream?"

She eventually relaxed. "Yeah. Burning Day again."

* * *

Chapter 39: It's Back

A cloudy day brought a somber mood as the invited guests gathered around the Goblin Fountain after breakfast. With the elderly pair of monkey mammals nowhere in sight, the crew of the Manessa Kwi, the three Education Service trainees, and a few others, all chatted about how they would handle what Jimox and Teina had endured in their lives.

Ashley would be deeply saddened if her civilization perished. Kolarrr'ka wouldn't shed a feather over it. T'sss'lisss had mixed feelings, and could relate to both attitudes.

Finally about noon, the honorary station hosts emerged from Fairy Castle, yawning and chatting with Brora. They slowly approached the fountain, but before even sitting down, the ursine healer's bracelet chimed urgently.

"Research ship Pena Belisana," an unseen avian voice squawked in haste, "just sent a broken transmission, saying something about a disease, and something burning, and requested approach guidance and landing instructions."

Jimox and Teina looked at each other with wide eyes, and decades of weariness suddenly melted from their shoulders. Jimox grabbed the healer's arm and tapped at her bracelet with his ancient furry fingers. "Rrr'tana, let us hear the entire transmission!"

After a short pause, the desperate call was replayed. "... entire crew affected ... passing continental beacon A-Four ... or is it B-Four? ... can hardly see straight ... contagious? ... burning ... should we land? ..."

The avian station host's voice returned. "That's it. I can't make contact again."

Teina blinked twice, then pulled the healer's arm close. "Rrr'tana, take direct ship control, and figure out where they are!"

"Working on it."

Jimox looked at Teina. "Let's get up to the control room!"

The pair steadied each other, then headed toward Fairy Castle at a pace they hadn't used in years. Brora was hard pressed to keep up.

Before going far, Teina turned her head but didn't stop walking. "Captain, we're going to need a ship."

Ilika glanced at his crew, and all six of them fell in behind the elderly couple and their healer.

*

The avian host made room at the station control desk as soon as Jimox and Teina hurried in. Teina paused to cough deeply, then mastered it by sheer force of will and sat down.

"Pena Belisana confirmed that the crew is sick," the bird reported, "and gave me control without question. It's about a thousand kilometers east, heading this way."

"They said . . . *burning* . . ." Teina muttered thoughtfully. "Seal the ship, Rrr'tana."

The bird glanced at Teina for a second, then issued voice commands for the research ship to switch to internal air, and not open any hatch without station approval.

The Pena Belisana, in a pleasant voice, confirmed the commands.

Ilika and the others could feel the tension, almost fear, that filled the room, so they stayed in the visitors' area of couches, planters, and low tables with racks of station maps and retreat pamphlets.

"We need to put them somewhere on the ground," Teina said. "Somewhere . . . they can't infect *anyone*."

"Kemlo," Jimox proposed.

With sweeps of his wings, Rrr'tana caused the continental map on the large display to zoom in until it showed just a small expanse of barren desert. Sand dunes and eroded badlands surrounded one labeled location at the center.

Jimox tapped at the console before him. "No guests right now, just a pair of equine hosts."

"Too close, biologically," Teina asserted.

Jimox looked at her and nodded.

Ilika whispered to Kibi, she tapped Mati on the shoulder, and the two slipped out the door.

Rrr'tana added overlays of current and historical surface winds, and all three hosts studied the display.

The avian pointed with his wing. "The wind can sometimes be from the southwest, but it's usually the same as today, straight off the ocean in the west. *Never* from the east."

"So there's no way it can get here," Teina observed, "and no one to infect for three thousand kilometers to the east. Let's do it."

Jimox turned around. "Captain, we need to evacuate the equine hosts and take them up to Deep Valley Springs, then return to Kemlo and deal with . . . what appears to be an outbreak of the disease that destroyed our civilization."

At that moment, the Manessa Kwi settled onto the ground just outside Fairy Castle.

*

The equine hosts of Kemlo Desert Retreat were fairly young, not very experienced, and quite shocked that they had a mere eight minutes to prepare to evacuate.

The male was mostly concerned with the retreat, but the female grabbed a bag, stuffed a few things in, and nudged her partner outside just as the deep-space response ship appeared over the range of mountains in the west.

Under ion drive, Mati had the Manessa Kwi over the retreat's landing area in seconds, and on the ground seconds later. Kibi raised the big table and re-arranged the seats to make room for two horses.

The hatch opened and the ramp appeared. The male looked back with worry at the tile roof, thick walls, and rounded arches of his desert retreat, his first assignment as a planet station host. His partner nipped him, and he bolted up the ramp and into the waiting ship.

The hatch closed, and two passenger seats swiveled to reveal Jimox and Teina, both working at knowledge pads with most of their attention, even as they greeted the young equines.

The hosts of Kemlo Desert Retreat had seldom had the honor of sitting with the legendary first hosts of Siminia Three Planet Station, so they instinctively bowed their heads in respect.

The elderly monkey mammals appeared not to notice. "Deep Valley Springs, please, Captain," Jimox said, looking up from his knowledge pad.

"Chart is up," Sata announced.

"Clear weather with mild thermal updrafts," Rini said.

"Ion one," Mati requested.

*

Green gardens and a swimming pool seemed out of place among endless kilometers of sand dunes, salt flats, and rocky hills.

The crew of the Manessa Kwi would have loved to linger, but Jimox and Teina were anxious to get back to Kemlo. The two equine passengers thanked Kibi, clopped down the ramp, and stood looking around, wondering what they would do here besides worry about their primary assignment, now a disease quarantine station.

As the little ship rose back into the air, a large spider emerged from the nearest tile-roofed building and offered to give the horses a tour.

*

"I haven't been able to get a coherent word out of the crew," Rrr'tana said, still working at the control desk back at the planet station. "The ship is on a slow final approach — let me know if you need more time."

"We'll be there in less than a minute," Sata reported.

Jimox shuddered for a moment and gripped Teina's hand tightly until he recovered. "Steward, please help us get every med kit on the ship into the airlock," he said firmly. "We don't yet know what we'll have to deal with." He stood, and helped Teina do the same. Their eyes held a mixture of excitement and fear.

Kibi turned and looked at Ilika. "Shouldn't someone else go, or just wait for healers from Satamia?"

Ilika let Teina answer.

"Kibi, we're immune to it, and we're the only two people in Satamia who can make that claim. We *think* felines and canines are also immune, but that theory hasn't been confirmed."

Kibi frowned, but followed them down the lift to help with medical kits. Just as she was descending, she heard Sata announce that the other ship was landing, and Ilika ordered Manessa to switch to internal air.

The avian host back at the planet station landed the plague ship just a few meters from the front door of Kemlo Desert Retreat. As soon as the hatch opened, a reptile staggered out, supporting an avian in even worse shape. Next, an ursine crawled down the ramp, and with Jimox' help, dragged himself in through the door. Finally a monkey mammal, somewhat different from Jimox and Teina, tried to come out alone, but collapsed halfway down the ramp. Teina moved as quickly as she could, but the sick crew member hit the ground hard.

As soon as Jimox settled the ursine inside, he rushed back out to help Teina with the monkey mammal, now only half-conscious.

That was the easy part, Jimox realized, as he stepped into the little research ship. Six specialists were under blankets in the passenger area, shivering and moaning, and two more crew members were found in their cabins on the lower deck, wishing they could die to end the terrible burning sensation racking their bodies.

The two elderly hosts, believing themselves immune to the disease, gave each crew member or researcher a stimulant, then helped them, one at a time, into the retreat.

As soon as the planet station host moved the plague ship, a small cargo carrier took its place and unloaded more medical supplies and equipment with a mechanical arm through the airlock.

For the next hour, the crew of the Manessa Kwi sat in their ship feeling completely useless.

Jimox and Teina reached inside themselves for reserves of energy and courage they had forgotten they possessed. They helped the sick crew and specialists into beds, attached nutrition feeds and medical monitors, paused to slurp down energy drinks, then went back to work. Jimox felt his blood pressure swinging wildly, and ignored it. Teina turned from her patients just long enough to cough until she nearly turned blue.

The medical monitors relayed their data to the nearby ships, and it flew instantly to Satamia Star Station. A team of healers studied it and sent back instructions for nutrition adjustments and further tests. Soon, they began to arrive at some conclusions.

The healers at the star station, and the pair of elderly hosts, began to realize the truth at about the same time.

The disease was virulent, airborne, highly-contagious, crossed from one species to another easily, and was quite deadly without intensive medical care.

It could easily become a plague.

But the victims had spoken of *burning* because of the painful fevers they were enduring, not because of any urge to set fire to things.

It was not the plague that had destroyed the former monkey-mammal civilization of Siminia Three.

And neither Jimox, nor Teina, were immune.

A ship full of healers and assistants dashed out of Satamia Star Station and jumped into star transit. Their destination: Kemlo Desert Retreat, direct.

✳ ✳ ✳

Chapter 40: The Biggest Decision

Time stood still.

All of the crew members and specialists from the plague ship were comfortable and stable, with healers at Satamia monitoring them.

Jimox and Teina trembled as they leaned on each other and looked around. Pride showed in their eyes. Avians, ursines, reptiles, and monkey mammals were all safe and likely to recover. Members of all those species, and others, had given countless years of service, and sometimes their very lives, to Siminia Three Planet Station over the previous two hundred years. That planet station and its retreats, created out of an old amusement park and a handful of resorts, were the closest things the elderly couple had to children.

Teina coughed deeply while Jimox held her close. When the fit finally passed, she struggled to find her voice, but only managed a whisper. "I can feel . . . fever starting. Our last mission, dear Jimox?"

He trembled, knowing the adrenaline rush of the emergency was wearing off. "I can feel it too. Yes, I think this was our last mission, dear Teina."

"I think . . . that's okay."

"Yes. I'm ready too. I don't think this old heart of mine would win against a new virus."

"Nor these old lungs of mine."

"Perhaps . . ." he began tenderly, "one more short journey? The sand dunes are only about a hundred meters outside the back door . . ."

"I would love to walk with you in the dunes, dear Jimox. As long as I can lean on you."

"You can, if I can lean on you . . ."

She giggled for a moment like a young girl. "I've always loved sand dunes."

Jimox chuckled with the spirit of a boy setting out on an adventure with a girl at his side. "Me too."

They made their way slowly out the back door of Kemlo Desert Retreat just as the ship full of healers landed in front.

* * *

Chapter 41: Freedom

Healers with breathing masks, knowing the virus could be managed even if one of them should get it, poured through the front door of Kemlo Desert Retreat. They quickly checked on the dozen patients. Nutrition feeds were refilled, drugs added, monitors checked, and bedding changed. They talked to the patients when they were conscious, and watched vital signs closely when they weren't. An arachnid of great healing experience watched over the entire operation, and stayed in constant contact with Satamia Star Station.

On the Manessa Kwi, everyone tried to relax — until Rini revealed that Jimox and Teina were in the sand dunes behind the retreat.

Ilika let his crew discuss their thoughts and feelings.

Kibi, at first, was adamant that Manessa should pick them up. The crew could wear breathing masks and be back at Satamia before the virus could affect any of them.

Sata agreed.

Boro hesitated, but nodded.

Rini remained silent.

Mati took a deep breath. "Since coming to Nebador, I've learned some things about helping people who don't want to be helped. This feels like one of those times when . . . it might not be the right thing to do."

✳

Inside the retreat, a similar discussion was taking place between the arachnid in charge and several young healers.

"If they wanted medical care, don't you think they would have stayed in the retreat," the spider pointed out, "where equipment and supplies were available?"

"Yes, but . . ." a reptile began, "what if the disease is affecting their ability to think clearly?"

"That's a possibility, but the fact that they walked into the dunes, on their own feet, says otherwise."

"Shouldn't we err on the side of caution?" a bird asked.

"In many other situations, yes," the spider answered. "But considering their age — nearly twice life-span for their species under planetary conditions — their frailty, and the accomplishments of their lives — now mostly far in the past — we must ask ourselves this: can we not let them die in peace? Must they dig their own graves and throw themselves in to convince us that they are ready to move on?"

The healers and assistants continued tending the research-ship crew and specialists, but all wore thoughtful expressions.

✳

After a long discussion — to which Ilika, to his delight, did not have to contribute — Kibi finally sighed. "Okay, I see. I guess if I was that old, and lucky enough to still have the love of my life at my side . . ." She glanced at Ilika and he smiled. ". . . I'd want to be able to go on a walk and, if it was our time, to die without anyone messing with us."

✳   ✳   ✳

Chapter 42: The Work of the Living

The healers practiced their craft, and all the patients were expected to recover. The monkey mammal who had fallen from the ramp had a concussion and a deep infected cut, in addition to the plague virus that all the rest were fighting, and would need the most care.

Only one healer, an avian, became infected, but she spotted the symptoms early, became a patient, and was quickly stabilized.

That evening after the sun went behind the mountains, the arachnid in charge of the make-shift medical clinic allowed a pair of avian healers to walk out into the dunes. Jimox and Teina had not gone far, and were curled up together as if sleeping peacefully, but were already nearly covered by sand.

The healers stood silently for a few minutes, placed a beacon, then returned to their work with the living.

The cargo ship escorted the research vessel back to Satamia Star Station for complete sterilization, and the Manessa Kwi returned to the planet station.

*

Rrr'tana the station host had been so busy with the emergency at Kemlo that little news had been announced. Two assistant hosts, a pair of highly-trained reptiles, were now running the station itself.

As the last light of evening faded from the sky, T'sss'lisss, Ashley, and Kolarrr'ka waited just outside the landing circle.

As soon as the Manessa Kwi landed, the crew told the three Education Service trainees what they knew. They all moped around the Goblin Fountain until finally, at almost midnight, Rrr'tana staggered out of Fairy Castle, shared the news of casualties and survivors, then dragged himself off to bed.

*

The following morning, out of habit, the crew and their three passengers gathered at the Goblin Fountain. One assistant host joined them, but had little news to share.

Ilika took a slow breath. "Our assigned task, of witnessing the final mortal days of the planetary prince and princess of Siminia Three, is over. No one — at least no one conscious and lucid — witnessed their final labor for their fellow Nebador citizens. Their last hour or two together was private, as they chose, and was their right."

Kibi, with tears in her eyes, nodded.

"Ashley, Kolarrr'ka, and T'sss'lisss," Ilika went on, "have essays to finish, and that may require some further experiences or interviews here at the planet station."

The snake and the bird nodded. Ashley appeared to be far away.

"I know the rest of you have some favorite places here, and perhaps some more exploring to do."

Rini, Boro, and Mati nodded weakly.

"Let's aim for another Satamia day, which is about six days here, but let me know if you need more time. Arantiloria tells me your essays have priority over anything but emergencies."

The three Education Service trainees chatted as they strolled toward the World Tree together, and agreed that six days should allow them to finish.

They were about to go their separate ways when they looked at each other. In the eyes of the other two, each one saw their own sadness reflected. Suddenly, they all wrapped coils, wings, and arms around each other and held tightly for a long minute.

✳

That afternoon, T'sss'lisss rested her head on a balcony railing in Olde Towne. She had slept little the night before, and now felt fuzzy-headed, so she just let thoughts and feelings slither through her mind, without trying to make sense of them.

The little balcony she was on had amused her when she found it, as the only door was fake and wouldn't open, leaving access only for avians and good climbers like herself.

Now she gazed across an open plaza of Olde Towne, and as she watched, she noticed Rrr'tana guiding a cart of cleaning supplies toward one of the toilet rooms. The bird called to see if anyone was within, and getting no answer, hung a purple symbol on a peg by the door and guided his cart in.

For the next quarter hour, T'sss'lisss pondered how different this was from her home planet, where social class and status were rigidly enforced. The highest-ranking administrator of a space port, or theme park, would never be caught *dead* cleaning a toilet room.

Suddenly, the fuzziness in her head cleared and thoughts started coming, so she slipped a knowledge pad out of her carry-bag and started dictating.

✳

The following day, after breakfast together in the Castle Kitchen, T'sss'lisss slithered away toward Machineland, and Kolarrr'ka and Ashley strolled together into Forestland.

They came to a dark cave-like opening in a simulated rock wall, and Ashley pulled climbing gloves from her day pack. "This is my task today."

"Bok," Kolarrr'ka began with worry in his voice, "it says *strong tail required*, and you don't have one . . ."

"Just the price of getting this essay of mine done. I'll either get it written, or die in the process."

"Bok," he said and wrapped his wings around the short but strong monkey mammal.

Ashley suddenly realized how much she wanted to live through this experience so she could continue to feel Kolarrr'ka's gentle wings around her, and T'sss'lisss' strong coils. "Don't worry, I'll be careful," she said into his soft feathers. "Remember, I was an athlete on my home planet."

He released her and nodded, but his eyes glistened with worry.

Once Ashley was gone, the bird waddled back into Castleland, but had to pull out a map, scribbled on a piece of paper, given in strictest confidence, before he could figure out where he was going.

*

Jimox and Teina had decided, at ages fourteen and eighteen by their reckoning, years before making contact with Nebador, to let some corners of Similand return to a wild state. Those wild corners sometimes included original Similand decorations and structures, even minor attractions.

Following his map, Kolarrr'ka first followed a tiny brick path that wound into the trees at the back of the Fairy Picnic Area. An equine, even an adult ursine, wouldn't have fit. It ended at a crawl-hole in a hedge.

Kolarrr'ka squatted down and looked in. The little passage appeared to go nowhere, but it matched the location on his map, so he stretched his feathered neck into the hole, and discovered it didn't end, but turned sharply.

Laying his wings flat along his body, he carefully waddled forward. Keeping head and neck out in front and knees bent, he managed the sharp turn while feeling only one painful twinge. Soon he was able to stand up again. Glancing back, he could see his missing feather stuck in the twigs.

The way was now easier, but Kolarrr'ka found himself in a completely wild forest with a meandering path roughly trimmed to allow passage. He started to glimpse figurines of fairy-tale characters from the previous monkey-mammal civilization, always faded, green with moss, and mostly hidden by leaves or cocooned in vines and stickers.

Although the path forked several times, Kolarrr'ka followed his map, and soon came to an old cabin of monkey-mammal size. The mossy roof was thick with small plants and mushrooms, and a single door and window allowed entrance and light. On the little porch, in a wooden chair, sat an ancient reptile with misty eyes.

"Greetings, young avian. I've been expecting you. I don't know why Rrr'tana thought I could help you with your essay — I'm just an old, long-retired, assistant station host — but I'll try."

*　*　*

Chapter 43: Essays

The day finally arrived, five days after Jimox and Teina walked into the sand dunes, when the three Education Service trainees declared themselves ready to read their first drafts.

✳

T'sss'lisss read hers right after breakfast. She presented the idea that everyone in Nebador, even the most highly-trained and honored citizens, helped with the little things, like cleaning toilet rooms. In contrast, she described the civilization on her home planet, advanced enough for inter-planetary travel, but primitive enough for nearly constant warfare and, of course, strict class boundaries. Many of her listeners nodded with understanding, including those from Sonmatia Three.

The snake concluded her essay by proposing that doing the dirty work, willingly and with joy, separated wise people from those who were merely intelligent, and it always would.

✳

Kolarrr'ka volunteered to present his essay that afternoon. He started by talking about something everyone knew, that being invited to work in the Nebador Services only happened to people who had gone through huge challenges and tests in their lives, and almost always a difficult journey of some kind.

Then he went on to consider the requirements for becoming planetary princes and princesses, a job so rare that no written rules existed. After talking to everyone he could find who knew Jimox and Teina personally, he concluded that it would not be possible for any mortals to do those jobs without first living through a planetary-wide catastrophic event. Only after that, could they possibly love their planet so much that they would gladly be responsible for it's welfare for the rest of time.

✳

That evening, Ashley was scared.

The last time she had read something aloud to a group of people, it was a silly little story about a boy and a monster. The audience had been her sixth-grade teacher and her fellow ten and eleven-year-old public school students.

Now she was almost fifteen — thirteen in the numbers of her home planet — and the people listening included the entire crew of a starship, the host of a planet station, a wise and powerful angel, her buddies T'sss'lisss and Kolarrr'ka who she thought were *both* smarter than her, and about twenty other Nebador citizens, all *much* smarter.

Ashley felt like she was out on a limb. Both of her fellow Education Service trainees, she knew, had written about ideas that were well-known in Nebador. The topic of Ashley's essay, on the other hand, was one she had never heard anyone talk about, nor seen anywhere in writing.

But now it was too late to change her mind and write her essay all over again.

As Ashley looked at the expectant faces around her, she wondered if she was about to flunk out of the Education Service. She took a deep breath.

"Real Recreation Requires Real Risk," she read with her heart in her throat. "That's . . . um . . . my tentative title. *Rrrr* for short."

Brora smiled.

She looked around at her audience. Kolarrr'ka was nodding thoughtfully. That allowed Ashley to breathe again, as she really liked and respected the bird, even though he was no older than she was.

Rini and T'sss'lisss appeared interested.

Ilika and Mati both smiled.

But what Ashley saw next allowed her to continue reading. Arantiloria was leaning forward, looking at her with respect, and nodding for Ashley to go on.

Ashley took a deep breath and looked at her knowledge pad. "On my home planet, no one is allowed to take risks. The laws are made by old people who are afraid of everything, so taking risks is against the law. We have theme parks, like this planet station once was, but everything is controlled by safety officers. When you finish visiting a theme park, you've learned nothing that wasn't in the brochure, you've experienced nothing that isn't in a video, and you aren't even tired — the safety officers made *sure* of that . . ."

✳ ✳ ✳

Chapter 44: The Celebration Begins

All during that day, Rrr'tana the station host stayed near the Goblin Fountain to listen and give encouragement. Those essays, he knew, were *the* most important thing happening at Siminia Three Planet Station that day . . . at least, during the daylight hours of that day.

No less than six, sometimes eight, assistant hosts were kept very busy sorting out the ships who arrived in a constant stream and needed landing instructions. Whenever a ship didn't need them, they hurried to squeeze extra beds into the hostels, hand out maps, or stock nutrition cabinets. By noon, they were fitting ships into unmarked spaces in the old Similand service areas. By the time Ashley read her essay that evening, the only available landing areas were outside the animal-proof fence.

Rrr'tana had complete confidence in all his well-trained assistant hosts.

✳

As evening light faded from the sky and Ashley neared the end of her essay, the assistant hosts directed the landing of the last ship, then closed the airspace over the planet station. One little ship didn't arrive in time, and was forced to divert to the parking lot of the old train station near downtown Westron. Fanators swooped northward at treetop level to fetch them.

" . . . so it is my conclusion that monkey mammals, and maybe all people, only keep growing until about age twelve, unless they have *real* problems to solve and *dangerous* challenges to face. If the problems and challenges are made-up, the young people know, and it doesn't work. With only made-up challenges — or none at all — they turn into what my planet calls *marshmallows* — soft, sweet, gooey things with no strength, no wisdom, and no personal power."

Ashley lowered her knowledge pad and breathed a huge sigh of relief as all her listeners smiled, clapped, shook their scales, or otherwise indicated that they had found her essay well worth hearing.

Just as the cheering died down, and Ashley realized she was parched and needed a carton of pinkfruit juice, maybe two or three, an explosion high above Fairy Castle turned all eyes toward the sky, where sparkles of many colors radiated and danced in the air before finally winking out.

Rrr'tana looked up and cooed.

Since accepting Ilika's offer of a ride to Satamia Star Station, Ashley had seen many different artistic lighting effects in the star and planet stations, and at the local universe capital itself. Some of them, she now knew, were made of light and other forms of energy, manipulated by the artist. Others were actually living beings, sometimes mortal, more often spiritual.

But as she gazed up at the darkening sky, felt the brush of T'sss'lisss' coils on one side, and Kolarrr'ka's feathers on the other, she knew she was seeing something different.

Just then an explosion, high above Machineland, sent sparkles of green, blue, and violet in all directions.

Ashley suddenly realized that these were real sparks, and she could even smell sulfur. If she remembered her universe history lessons, only monkey mammals ever used fire to make such lighting effects.

"Fireworks," she whispered.

T'sss'lisss looked at her, head cocked.

"These are real, old-fashioned, monkey-mammal fireworks!" Ashley explained.

Kolarrr'ka joined the conversation. "I don't think the crew of the Manessa Kwi had anything to do with it, and I know that *you've* had your beak in a knowledge pad for days."

Ashley laughed as red and yellow sparks danced over Olde Towne.

"Jimox and Teina ... the planetary prince and princess ..." T'sss'lisss proposed.

"Of course!" Ashley agreed.

Kolarrr'ka fluffed up his feathers. "They must have recalled a fond memory from childhood, and given the specs to Nebador technicians to create ... what did you call them? Fireworks? ... for this occasion."

Ashley hugged the bird tightly for a moment, then turned to the snake and did the same. "What a wonderful gift, right after reading my essay! It's almost as if they were watching me, and timed it perfectly!"

"Do you have any doubt?" T'sss'lisss asked, peering at Ashley with reptilian eyes that reflected the fireworks in the sky.

✻

While the crew, trainees, and a few others watched the fireworks from the Goblin Fountain, musicians were setting up in the Castleland Plaza, and dancers began to gather.

Kibi quickly noticed, and her ears told her that more musicians, in other parts of the planet station, were already playing.

A moment later, the doors to the Castle Kitchen were flung open wide. Reptiles and ursines carried tables outside, and countless trays of food and drink followed.

More lights came on all across Castleland to dispel the evening darkness, and soon Nebador citizens began to prowl every path on bicycles, wagons, tricycles, skate boards, and occasionally their own feet or hooves.

✻

One empty wagon, pulled by a large, furry ape, came to a stop near the Goblin Fountain. "Personal taxi for Rini!" the ape announced.

He grinned at Mati, and she grinned back and gave him a shove toward the wagon.

A strong equine, wearing a saddle, clopped up to the fountain. "Personal transport for Brora!"

The bear's eyes sparkled with delight as she climbed onto the horse's back.

A fanator landed. "Personal flight service for T'sss'lisss!"

She nodded to her two friends, then slithered into the riding harness.

"We have to stay below forty meters because of the fireworks," the fanator explained as it took off.

More wagons, equines, and bicycle-driven carriages arrived, and it wasn't long before Rrr'tana stood alone at the Goblin Fountain. Several visitors had volunteered to give him rides, but he had stood his ground, declaring that *someone* had to keep an eye on the planet station.

However, after checking on the assistant host on duty in the control room, he was thinking that he just might wander over to the dance in Olde Towne where some very talented ursines were playing.

Sata's taxi was a small open carriage with a reptilian cyclist behind. He was forced to pedal very slowly because the planet station was filled with people dancing, eating, or just gazing up at the fireworks. Sata laughed aloud, realizing she could easily walk faster.

Five outdoor dance areas throbbed with music, and Sata wanted to try them all. Her cyclist joined in each dance, but was ready and willing when Sata wanted to move on. Sometimes she spotted Kibi twirling up a storm, or Ashley using some of her gymnastics prowess. At other dance areas, she didn't know anyone personally, but felt comfortable jumping into any group dance, or grabbing a partner of any species or gender.

For a moment, she remembered when musicians would play in the marketplace of the capital city of her old kingdom, and how quickly she would have landed in slavery if she had ever been so bold.

Kolarrr'ka felt guilty as soon as he climbed into the red wagon.

The golden-haired ursine had only pulled him about a hundred meters when the bird declared that he could only allow this to continue if they could trade off.

The bear's eyes took on a glint of humor, and she gestured for Kolarrr'ka to take the handle of the wagon.

Bird stepped out and bear climbed in.

Kolarrr'ka slipped his neck through the handle, then pulled with all his might, but could not budge the little wagon with its ursine cargo, sitting up with arms crossed and a smug look, waiting for her ride.

Eventually the bird gave up, caught his breath, and sighed. "I . . . bok . . . failed to take into account the great difference in weight."

The bear smiled. "Also, your largest muscles are for your wings, which don't help in this situation."

The bird nodded. "I'm sorry."

"No apology needed. You're in the *Education* Service, one of the hardest jobs in the universe. All I have to do is analyze planetary geology and predict future tectonic activity — child's play really. And by the way, I can barely tell the difference between the empty wagon and the wagon with one medium-size bird in it. *Now* will you let me pull you?"

Kolarrr'ka ducked his head. "Bok."

In Machineland, the bird and bear found music that inspired them to stop. Kolarrr'ka glimpsed Ashley dancing and T'sss'lisss on her fanator overhead, but mostly the avian was in a thoughtful mood, content to watch the celebration and sample the many kinds of food and drink.

He pondered his essay, and wondered if he would ever know for sure what qualities and circumstances could make a planetary prince and princess. He remembered the ancient reptile in the little mossy cabin deep in a forgotten corner of the planet station, and wanted to visit him once more before leaving.

And as much as he was enjoying the company of his new ursine friend, Kolarrr'ka felt amazement — and happiness — about the deep bond he was forming with his fellow trainees T'sss'lisss and Ashley.

* * *

Chapter 45: Planetary Prince and Princess

Jimox and Teina noticed that the musicians in Forestland were playing in a different key from those in Machineland, and the tempo of the music under the World Tree completely clashed with the band in the Olde Towne Plaza. But they thought nothing of it, since none of their guests, except maybe T'sss'lisss on fanator-back, could hear more than one group of musicians at a time.

From the couple's new perspective, high above Castleland, above even the fireworks, they looked down at the thousands of Nebador people having fun. Seeing their friends dancing and playing made them as happy as they could ever remember being, and they twirled around each other to whatever melody or rhythm caught their fancy from one moment to the next.

A purple glow appeared nearby.

"Welcome, Arantiloria!" Teina said with her new strong voice that did not require lungs.

"Greetings, Planetary Sovereigns! Everyone is enjoying the fireworks, with the possible exception of the fanators."

Jimox chuckled. "Please give them our apologies, and tell them we promise not to do it very often."

"I already did."

"Kerloran said we get an advisor," Teina said. "Will that be you?"

"No, I have my hands full with the monkey mammals of the Manessa Kwi, and they have some hard missions coming up. Your advisor will be far more experienced than I, and you'll meet her at Kerusemia once you start taking classes."

"Oh yeah, those," Jimox said with humor in his voice. "I guess we can't expect to be planetary prince and princess without knowing a thing or two."

Arantiloria laughed. "You would have done a better job than most mortals even in your youth when you first met!"

"Wow," Teina breathed. "I was seven years old. Now I'm two hundred and twenty three!"

Arantiloria embraced them both for a moment. "I'm going to check on my charges. Sata is in danger of wearing herself out before the party's half-over. If you've shot off enough fireworks, there are some folks here who would love to join the celebration." She gestured to the northern edge of the planet station.

A few hundred small, faint, shimmering shapes danced in the air just outside the old animal-proof fence. Most were blue or bright green, and some almost pure white. Only a few had tinges of yellow.

Teina glowed with happiness. "The ghosts!"

"I didn't know there were that many left on the whole planet!" Jimox declared as they both instantly swooped to the edge of the station and welcomed the little spirits in.

The ghosts all had voices that Jimox and Teina could hear clearly now, and several started chattering at once. Jimox listened as he moved with them back toward the middle of the planet station, but Teina hesitated, noticing something near the ground.

A single dull-green ghost moved about shyly, muttering to itself, not daring to come near the fence. Teina watched, unsure what to do. She noticed the dull green color occasionally separate into the brighter green of life and the yellow of confused emotion, then return to the sickly dull green again.

Jimox joined her and looked down. "What do you think?"

"I'm wondering if maybe one of a planetary princess's jobs might be to . . . you know . . . reach out to pathetic little beings like that when . . . um . . . they're ready."

Jimox thought about it. "It *is* hovering near the fence, implying it would like to come in. It's alone. It appears to be trying to separate out the feelings that are keeping it stuck."

Teina watched a while longer.

"And," Jimox added, "I think the whole point of being a planetary princess is that *you* have to decide what the job is all about. Nebador has a million classes they want us to take, and we get an advisor, but they never said they'd tell us what to do. Remember how Arantiloria greeted us? Planetary *Sovereigns*."

Teina thought a little longer, then suddenly turned toward the planet station and called in her strong voice, "I need a ghost volunteer!"

Three hundred and forty-six ghosts instantly lined up before her.

"I need someone who has learned patience and compassion . . ."

Most of the little spirits changed colors and backed up a few meters, leaving five.

". . . someone willing to be a companion to this guilty one who is trying to make some progress."

The five looked down. Four shrank away, leaving one.

✳

With hundreds of ghosts now glowing or sparkling all around the planet station, Jimox and Teina decided to save the rest of the fireworks for another occasion.

The fanators were relieved.

The hours passed, midnight came and went, and the crowds of Nebador citizens dancing and playing thinned out as they began yawning, parting with friends, and wandering toward beds in ships or hostels.

Looking down, the planetary sovereigns could easily see Ilika and Kibi snuggling on a bench in Olde Towne, Mati and Rini sharing a slow couples' dance in Forestland, and Sata placing a piece of candy on Boro's tongue at a serving table in Machineland. Teina spotted Kolarrr'ka, T'sss'lisss, and Ashley in the Crow's Nest of the World Tree, gazing around them at the well-lit sights and sounds of Siminia Three Planet Station, and the darkness beyond, once a sprawling city, now completely reclaimed by Nature, save for an occasional ruin.

A small white glow suddenly appeared nearby.

"Kasssor-k'm!" Jimox recognized easily. "We were planning to visit you at your little shack once the party was over!"

Teina embraced their first assistant host. "No more reptile body?"

"It wasn't much good anymore," he admitted. "It couldn't see past the porch railing, and scales kept falling off. I decided this was a good time to let go of it."

"You are more than welcome here, old friend!" Jimox declared. "We're going to need all the help we can get figuring out what to do with this planet of ours!"

"I'd be happy to help, but I only get a short visit right now, then I have to head to Kerusemia for classes and whatever else they decide I need to do. But my guide says it's always a pleasure to take up a Nebador citizen who doesn't have to start with the very basics."

Teina lowered her voice. "There's a guilty ghost here right now, and we paired it with an advanced one who appears to be following Giona's path.

Arantiloria is helping us keep an eye on them."

"That'll be good experience for the advanced one, at least," Kasssor-k'm speculated. "I miss Giona, and will look her up as soon as I have some free time."

"That avian Education Service trainee found you, I believe?" Jimox inquired.

The smaller spirit glowed brighter. "He's nice, and has good insights into some of the less-common universe workings. Oops, my guide is calling, have to go see if there's anything I *didn't* learn being an assistant host for a hundred and three years!"

They all embraced.

"See you soon, old friend!"

"Be well!"

✳

Of course neither Jimox and Teina, nor the ghosts, became tired or bored as the hours passed, but as dawn light crept into the eastern sky, few mortals remained awake in the planet station below.

Teina sighed, seeing that only one band, under the World Tree, continued to softly play. Most serving tables were nearly empty, and only a handful of wagons and tricycles still roamed the plazas and walkways.

Jimox smiled when he spotted Sata dancing with two avians. Boro was asleep on a bench nearby.

The three Education Service trainees, snake, bird, and human, could be seen leaning on each other as they slowly crossed the Forestland Plaza toward a hostel.

"Party's about over," Jimox said with a hint of sadness.

"Yeah, but *I* don't feel sleepy," Teina teased.

"*You're* not mortal anymore!"

Teina laughed.

Suddenly, they both became aware that Melorania urgently needed somewhere to put a thousand barely-sapient equines.

They looked at each other.

"I bet an island would be best, lots of grass, and without any other horses or donkeys," Teina speculated.

Jimox searched his memory, which now seemed to include details about every corner of Siminia Three. "I can think of several possibilities."

"Let's go look at them, then pick one!"

Without anyone on the ground being aware of it, Teina and Jimox left their beloved planet station for the first time, as planetary prince and princess, to respond to the needs of the universe.

Melorania instantly sent a flight objective to the transport ship in orbit around a planet that had just become unlivable for land animals. The steward and his staff of cooks and servers, not currently prepared to feed a thousand wild horses, were quite relieved.

✳

Ashley could feel T'sss'lisss, draped over her shoulders, alternately lift her head, then relax and give in to sleep. At Ashley's side, Kolarrr'ka seemed to be already asleep, but somehow his legs kept moving. Ashley knew, however, that those legs had no idea where they were going, so she kept a gentle arm around him.

The bird on duty at the entrance to the hostel startled awake. "Bok. It was full, but someone's mission collar chimed a little while ago . . . yes here it is, the last bed. None of you are very big . . . will you share?"

Kolarrr'ka shook himself awake, then looked at T'sss'lisss and Ashley.

Ashley nodded. "We'll get more sleep on a bed than in the passenger seats on the Manessa Kwi."

T'sss'lisss looked too sleepy to care.

Kolarrr'ka thought for a moment, then climbed onto the bed, near the middle, and turned his head to rest it on his own back.

Ashley curled around him, then blew a puff of air to removed a feather from her face.

T'sss'lisss coiled completely around the other two, relaxed, and was instantly asleep.

"That's one full bed," the host muttered as he returned to the door and his own dreams.

*　*　*

Chapter 46: Heading Home

The day after the great celebration, Rrr'tana the station host found Kasssor-k'm's body on the porch of his little shack. As soon as others started waking and getting some breakfast, he asked for helpers.

Every assistant host who could be spared from essential duties, and dozens of station visitors, grabbed brush-cutting tools and began enlarging the path to the little cabin and cleaning out that entire weedy corner of old Similand.

Kolarrr'ka quickly volunteered, and found Ashley and T'sss'lisss at his side. They helped Rrr'tana with the cabin itself, going through the legendary reptile's meager belongings to decide what was trash and what should remain to give visitors some idea of how Jimox and Teina's faithful helper spent the final years of his life.

The following day, *The Roofers* arrived, scraped off the moss, and gave the little cabin a coating of protection against the centuries ahead.

That evening, as orange sunset light made the cabin's old wood seem to glow, everyone in the station who had known Kasssor-k'm shared their memories from the little porch as hundreds of visitors listened.

The planetary prince and princess smiled.

*

At about the same time, the last patients at Kemlo Desert Retreat were recovering and being transferred to Satamia Star Station. A ship arrived to give the place a thorough cleaning, and another to study the disease and determine its possible future dangers.

Although the equine hosts would have been willing to return to Kemlo, they whinnied with joy when asked if they'd like to become the hosts at Snowy Mountain Hot Springs, a thousand kilometers farther north.

A new Nebador monument was commissioned, to be numbered four hundred and thirty-five of those on Siminia Three, and placed at Jimox and

Teina's last resting place. It would tell the story of their final labors for their fellow citizens, and their choice to gracefully let go of mortal life, at that place, and take up their duties as planetary sovereigns.

In the days that followed, many of the ships at Siminia Three Planet Station started getting assignments, and some crew members and passengers had to return to the star station for classes. The planet station slowly returned to its usual assortment of twenty or thirty visiting ships.

Ilika noticed that his crew was starting to spend time at their primary consoles, running diagnostics and otherwise making sure their little ship was ready to go. The three Education Service trainees also seemed to find little else they wanted to do at the planet station.

As they all gathered at the table in the passenger area for a simple midday meal, Boro wore a thoughtful expression. "Ilika . . . I was just noticing . . . all our missions seem to have something to do with *death*. Will we ever have missions that are just about . . . you know . . . lighter things?"

Arantiloria appeared and took a seat, clearly interested in how the captain was going to answer that difficult question. All the crew members and trainees looked at Ilika.

He leaned back to ponder his response. He knew very well that Arantiloria could answer the question much better than he could, but that no force in the universe could get him out of the hot seat Boro had put him in.

After one more deep breath, he began.

"Sapient planetary societies can — and must — handle most of their own problems. They usually try every possible trick to *avoid* doing so, but eventually realize that no one is going to help them, except in a few rare situations that aren't their fault . . ."

"Like the supernova and the bunnies," Mati remembered.

"Right. There are many, many challenges that most sapient species successfully handle. The ones they most often *fail* to handle, and that sometimes lead to their complete destruction, like happened here, are those challenges that involve birth and death."

He looked at Arantiloria, whose penetrating gaze almost made his head spin, but he didn't see any displeasure, so far, in her angelic expression.

"What is it about birth and death," Rini began, "that make them so hard to handle?"

Ilika looked at Kibi.

She was able to answer without even thinking. "Fear."

Ilika nodded. "When something stirs primal fears, all the rational thinking skills that have been developed over thousands of years go out the window. The species loses touch with reality. There have been planets where they thought they could go on having babies, doubling their population every few decades, even though their own scientists calculated that they would soon fill the universe with the mass of their bodies . . ."

Everyone in the room snickered or laughed at the absurd notion.

"Of course, it never works. Death through disease and war always limits the population. Here on Siminia Three, the government thought it could create biological weapons that would kill their kind without, you know, killing their kind."

Sata sighed. "And with the passing of Jimox and Teina, they're all gone."

Ilika nodded. "So our missions will often involve death of some kind because that's the one thing, along with birth at the other end of the same life cycle, that most mortals can't think clearly about. That doesn't mean we'll pull their asses out of the fire in very many situations, but it does mean that *death*, in some form, will often be involved."

"And getting trapped in the ice on Sonmatia Seven was part of our training for that," Mati speculated, looking at Arantiloria.

Although she hadn't yet been assigned as their training specialist at that time, she had examined the records of the event in all possible detail. "Yes," she said, "but you came from a world in which death was always close. That gave you a big head start."

✴

The crew and trainees took the rest of that day to enjoy their favorite parts of the planet station one last time. All pleasantly tired, they got a good night's sleep, then woke up early and made a hearty breakfast.

"Sata, you have command for our return trip home," the captain said from the head of the table.

After making crew assignments and seeing that all the breakfast dishes were done, Sata took the command chair and everyone else got comfortable at their stations or in passenger seats.

"Siminia Three control," Kibi began from the navigator's station, "Manessa Kwi at landing site C-Seventeen requests departure instructions."

"Good morning, Manessa Kwi!" a young reptilian voice responded. "Careful ascent to one hundred meters, then slow eastbound past the inner marker. Watch for fanators. Moderate speed to the outer marker."

Rrr'tana's voice jumped in. "Good journey to you, Manessa, crew, and passengers! You all have a special place in our hearts now, as you were witnesses to the greatest transition this planet has ever known. We look forward to your next visit!"

At that moment, a single small firework exploded high above the World Tree, causing red and green sparks to dance for a few seconds.

The crew and passengers of the little ship smiled or laughed, and few eyes were dry as they remembered the final mortal days of Teina and Jimox, the last two monkey mammals of Siminia Three.

Eventually Sata got serious. "Okay … we're going to pretend we just joined the monastery in the mountains. No talking until we get to Satamia, unless an emergency comes up."

In the passenger area, Ashley leaned forward. "This could be interesting."

"Yesss."

"Bok."

* * * * *

The Magic Needle

by Kathleen Tully

This story depicts the future of Risan Gor after her rescue by the crew of the Manessa Kwi, at Melorania's direction, near the end of *Book Four: Flight Training*.

Timod Gor's gold didn't last long. He drank up some of it, smoked some, bought whores with a lot, gave some away to impress people, and gambled. He was at the card table when he ran out of gold, and thought he had a good hand, so he bet his daughter. He lost the hand, but suddenly sobered up enough to realize what he had done and refused to give her to the winner. The winner didn't like being cheated, a dagger flashed out, and even before Timod Gor hit the floor, little Risan Gor ran out into the black night faster than anyone could follow.

She didn't touch her gold, still hidden on the hill, for a long, long time. It felt dirty because it had made her father stupid with drink and smoke and gambling. So she just walked, and when she saw people on the road, she hid in the bushes until they were close enough to tell if they were good people or bad.

Most of the time, the people were good when she thought they were. She asked if she could work for her food. Sometimes they said yes. Sometimes they were too poor and had to say no. Sometimes they were bad and she had to run again. Luckily she was too young for them to care much about catching.

*

For two years she worked doing anything people wanted her to. Slowly she discovered she was best at sewing, because she had long, nimble fingers, and she liked doing it. So when she came to a new village or farm, she started saying she was a seamstress. Often enough to keep her fed, they needed one.

Risan Gor was eight, and getting really good at sewing, when she started saving up some copper pieces. One day she saw some fancy new iron needles in the marketplace, and the woman said they lasted a lot longer than bone needles. The girl dug into her money pouch and counted out the precious coins.

By the time she was nine, she would arrive in a town and people would start whispering, "It's Risan the Seamstress! Tell the innkeeper! He's got lots of mending to do!" Soon she had copper AND silver pieces in her pouch, and half a dozen iron needles, of different shapes and sizes, in her shoulder bag along with *four* colors of thread. She still kept the bone needles, just to remember her younger days.

✳

The years passed, and Risan the Seamstress liked to go on walks in the woods when she wasn't sewing. She was eleven when she found a pretty, shiny rock, so she put it into her bag. Back in her tiny one-room workshop, the shiny rock was sitting on the work table when she happened to toss an iron needle near it. The needle jumped, and stuck to the rock!

She nearly ran to the blacksmith.

"Sir, what kind of rock is this? My iron sewing needles stick to it!"

"Hmm. I've heard of these. Some kind of strange iron that fell from the sky, some say. I can't think of any use for it." He tossed the rock back to her.

She couldn't think of any use for it either, so she just used it on her work table to hold her needles.

✳

Risan was twelve when she happened to drop her smallest iron needle, the one she used for embroidery, into a cup of water. The needle floated on the surface of the water, and quickly pointed toward the shiny rock, only about a foot away. She looked at it for a minute, then dried it off and went back to sewing.

About a month later, she set down her smallest needle after some embroidery work that left her fingers sore, and was about to take a drink of water. She looked at the needle and the cup of water, and remembered the first time. But this time was different. She had taken the shiny rock to show a friend, and had accidentally left it there. *What would the needle do*, she wondered, *without the rock near? Would it point toward her friend's house?*

She carefully dropped the needle into the water, and it floated, just like the first time. It started slowly swinging to point at something, but it wasn't her friend's house. She stepped outside to make sure. Yep, she was right — her friend's house was a different direction.

This new thing she had discovered was funny, but she couldn't think of any use for it, so she went back to sewing.

*

Risan the Seamstress started dreaming about whatever the needle was pointing to when the shiny rock wasn't near. She could never quite see it, so far away and shrouded in mist in the dream. But she woke up curious.

Her twelfth year was passing into her thirteenth when she could stand it no longer. She was, honestly, getting tired of dreaming about pointing needles. A dream about a handsome young man, now and then, would be nice.

She started putting a small wooden cup and her embroidery needle into her shoulder bag whenever she went walking. At the town well, just a block from her house, she got a cup of water, found a place to sit where no one could see, and put the needle in. It pointed straight back to her workshop, where the rock sat on the table.

But at the stream outside of town, it slowly went a different way again. At the river two miles away, it did the same thing. At three other places, all a mile or more away from the village, the needle pointed to . . .

"Sir," she asked an old man pulling his little boat onto the riverbank, "are you a sailor?"

"Was when I was young and strong. Sailed the five seas for twenty years."

"So you know how to tell directions?"

"Sure do! On most ships, I was the closest thing they had to a navigator."

"Can you tell me what direction it is to that mountain that looks like a bird's beak?"

"Buzzard's Peak, that's called. Every sailor 'round here knows *that* direction, 'cause it's right under the North Star, the star that all the Heavens rotate around. That's *north*, little lady, about as perfect as anyone can tell."

*

Risan the Seamstress was fourteen when she started remembering something that had happened to her at age five. She remembered a journey by ship, then bad weather, and finally a very cold place with ice in every direction, even floating on the sea.

For some reason, the way she and her father had been rescued was hard to remember. She didn't *want* to remember what came next — her father drinking and smoking and gambling, then getting killed and leaving her alone. But her mind kept wandering back to the voyage by ship, and she started remembering voices.

"What do you *mean* you don't know which direction to go?" the captain bellowed.

"I haven't been able to see the stars for days!" the frightened man whined. "North could be that way, or that way, or . . ."

The conversation ended when the captain thrust a dagger between the navigator's ribs.

Risan brought her mind back to the present, ripped out a couple of stitches she had gotten in the wrong place because of daydreaming, and mumbled to herself, "He must not have had a magic needle. He must not have even *known* about magic needles."

In the days that followed, she started to wonder if maybe that strange rock of hers had a use after all.

*

She was fifteen when she realized several things at about the same time, and thinking about them nearly made her sick. She wasn't pretty enough to catch the eye of any of the handsome young men. She didn't know how to do anything but sew. And her hands were becoming stiff and sore, more and more quickly, while she worked. It the stiffness kept getting worse, in just a few years she'd be unable to sew enough to pay the rent and buy food.

A month later, she quit taking new sewing jobs, finished the ones she was working on, packed a bag, and walked out the door before paying the rent that was due. She took her strange, shiny rock, a few small iron needles, one spool of thread, and a wooden cup, but little else. She was not planning to set up a new sewing business somewhere else. She was casting herself into the wind to see what the world would show her.

After a week of travel, she was wandering along the docks of the port city of her kingdom. At first she was lost in her thoughts, but slowly started to realize that something was wrong. There were four great sailing ships in the harbor, but no cargos were being loaded or unloaded. Each had a man or two standing guard, but nothing else was happening. She became curious and approached one of the ships.

"Hey there, sailor! What news from the sea?"

"You watch your tongue, young woman, for I be not some lousy sailor, but am truly the *captain* of this proud vessel . . . for all the good it does me."

"Why would a captain speak in such tones? Is she not a fair ship that races before the wind?"

"She would be, if she had any work to do. Now . . . she just rots in the harbor, and neither she, nor I, like it much."

Risan the ex-seamstress got comfortable on a crate at the edge of the wharf. "What keeps her from having work, if I may ask. I am without work right now out of choice, but not you, I take it."

"Certainly not! I'd be hauling cargos back and forth across the sea if anyone dared send them anymore. It's in my blood. I can do nothing else. If I cannot sail, I might as well lie down and die."

"Why do they not send cargos?"

"Too many ships lost. Too much bad weather. Hardly half get to the far shore. Some, they say, end up at the bottom of the world where there is nothing but ice. Most are never seen again. One made it back from there, a few years ago, and told of the bones of ships scattered on the ice and the bones of men piled on the shore."

Risan swallowed. "I've been there," she said softly.

"Have ye? Well, you're one of the few who can say that and still draw breath to boast of it."

She was thoughtful for a while. "What would be your chances of getting across the sea safely if you had something … something magical … that always pointed north?"

His eyes grew very large. "My stars, I'd be the luckiest captain in the kingdom! I'd be able to guide the helmsman true even in the worst storm or fog! But such a magical thing does not exist, does it?"

"It does, and I have one."

"Well, you come right aboard, young woman, and I shall make you … you don't mind soup and bread, do you?"

"I love soup and bread. I was a seamstress, nothing fancy."

*

They talked for hours, ate soup and bread, drank ale, and became friends. But the captain still frowned whenever the talk circled around to his ship once again carrying cargos.

"What bothers you?" Risan asked.

"It takes more than a ship and a magical north-finder. It takes a patron."

"What's that?"

"An investor, a rich man who *believes* the voyage will be successful, believes it enough to put up the four or five great gold pieces for a crew, supplies, and a cargo to sell on the far shore. After so many ships lost, there's hardly a patron to be found. And believe me, Risan, me saying I know a young woman with a magical north-finder, an unproven gadget no one's ever heard of, is not going to shake even a *copper* piece out of anyone's money pouch, much less the gold that would be needed. So unless *you* know of a patron who would take such a risk …"

Her mind went back ten years and struggled to remember something … something about gold … gold that her father didn't know about. She glimpsed, in her memory, a shaggy black-haired … lady? … angel? … burying something … a metal tube with something very heavy inside. She saw the log the angel-lady put over the hiding place. She saw the hill it was on from the road to the village.

"How far is it from here to Tolek?" she asked the captain.

"That little sheep and cattle village in the hills? Half a day on a horse, or a long day's walk."

"I think I know … a patron there who … would believe in my north-finder. What does a patron get for his risk?"

"If the voyage is successful, he gets his money back and *at least* another great gold, sometimes two, depending on how well the cargo sells. And with so few ships making it, I *know* the cities across the sea will pay good money for our wares."

Risan Gor ate her soup and bread silently for a little while longer.

"I'm going on a little journey. If I find … the patron … I'll be back in … two or three days with five great gold pieces. Will you be here?"

He grinned, pulled her close, and kissed her.

* * *

Note from J. Z. Colby: It is true that the compass was already in use in the kingdom that is the setting of *NEBADOR Books One*, *Two*, and *Three*, but this story takes place in a different kingdom. It is often the case in history that inventions come to one part of a world before, sometimes long before, another. Even more strange are those moments in history when discoveries are made at multiple locations at about the same time, but without any cross-influence.

About the Authors

Born in the Mojave Desert, J. Z. Colby now lives and writes deep in a forest of the Pacific Northwest.

He has studied many subjects, formally and informally, including psychology, philosophy, education, and performing arts, but remains a generalist. His primary profession as a mental health counselor, specializing with families and young adults, gives him many stories of personal growth, and the motivation to develop his team of young critiquers and readers.

All his life, he has been drawn toward a broad understanding of human nature, especially those physical, emotional, mental, and spiritual situations in which our capacity to function seems to reach its limits. He finds fascinating those few individuals who can transcend the limits of our common human nature and the dictates of our cultures.

In his spare time, he flies helicopters and airplanes.

He may be contacted at the email address listed on the internet site www.nebador.com.

Kathleen Tully, 16, lives in Iowa, and loves inventions and discoveries of all kinds. She was identified as highly gifted years ago, is studying every kind of science she can get her hands on in high school, and is preparing to apply to colleges.

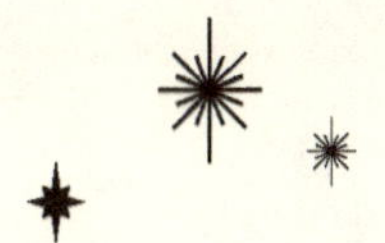

9 781936 253760